I ♥ Band!

Sleepovers, Solos, and Sheet Music

I ♥ Band!

Sleepovers, Solos, and Sheet Music

by Michelle Schusterman

Grosset & Dunlap
An Imprint of Penguin Group (USA) LLC

GROSSET & DUNLAP
Published by the Penguin Group
Penguin Group (USA) LLC, 375 Hudson Street, New York, New York 10014, USA

USA | Canada | UK | Ireland | Australia | New Zealand | India | South Africa | China

penguin.com
A Penguin Random House Company

Cover illustration by Genevieve Kote.

Library of Congress Cataloging-in-Publication Data is available.

ISBN 978-0-448-45685-0 10 9 8 7 6 5 4 3 2 1

To bus trips, breakdowns,
and Billy Madison

The second half of seventh grade should come with some sort of warning: *Congratulations! You're exactly halfway through middle school, so everything's about to get twice as hard*.

Apparently all my teachers came back from winter break last month thinking we were high-schoolers or something. My English teacher, Mr. Franks, announced that we'd be writing two essays a week—two!—*plus* a big research paper due later this semester. In science, Mrs. Driscoll had given us a crazy schedule for our science fair projects, and our labs were getting ridiculous—as if any day now she'd be asking us to find a cure for the common cold. And the way Mr. Hernandez kept drilling us on verb conjugations, I was pretty sure he was expecting us to be fluent in Spanish by the end of the year.

But that was nothing compared to band.

My music folder was *stuffed*: a thick packet full of

new scales and exercises; "Labyrinthine Dances"—this ridiculously hard piece that we'd been rehearsing since the beginning of the year for a contest that wasn't even until April; three more songs we'd be performing on our band trip to New Orleans a month from now; my music for the all-region concert in a few weeks, which sent a flurry of butterflies flitting around my stomach every time I looked at it; and "Pastorale for Horn," my solo for Solo and Ensemble Competition, which I'd perform in front of a judge for a rating and (hopefully) a medal.

As if all that wasn't enough, now Mr. Dante was handing out even *more*.

"'Triptych,'" he said, reaching across the saxes to hand me a sheet of music. "Brass trio—this one will be Holly, Aaron, and Liam. Next up, let's see . . . 'Canon in A,' woodwind quartet: Julia, Sophie, David, and Luis."

While Mr. Dante continued handing out parts, I stared at my music. The butterflies started swing dancing.

"Triptych" made all those other songs look like "Three Blind Mice."

"Wicked," Gabby said next to me, and I glanced at her music. It looked just as hard as mine, but Gabby could totally handle it. She was amazing.

I mean, I was good, too. I was actually first chair French horn in the advanced band. But still . . .

"When exactly is Solo and Ensemble again?" I asked her, even though I knew the answer.

"Last weekend of February," Gabby replied. "Right before the band trip."

"Less than a month," I said, drumming my fingers on the bell of my horn. "We have less than a *month*."

On my other side, Natasha Prynne was staring at her own music, her eyes wide. "This is crazy."

"I know," I agreed. Honestly, I was kind of relieved that she was worried, too. Up until all-region auditions last November, Natasha had been first chair in our section. Then I'd made the top all-region band, while Natasha was in the second band. And even though I practiced a *lot*, part of me still thought it was some sort of fluke. I was a really good horn player, but Natasha was pretty fantastic, too.

Someone tapped me on the shoulder, and the smell of cologne made my stomach flip for an entirely different reason.

"Hey, Holly, do you think we could practice this before school?" Aaron Cook asked, and I saw he was holding the trumpet part to "Triptych." "I had baseball tryouts yesterday, and it looks like practice is going to be pretty much every day after school for the next month or so."

"Sure!" I said, trying not to sound too enthusiastic. "How about Wednesdays and Fridays?"

"Works for me," Aaron replied. "I'll check with Liam." He smiled at Natasha. "So who's in your ensemble?"

Natasha half-turned in her chair to face him. "Um,

Gabe, Victoria, and . . . I think Max." Her voice was a little higher than normal.

"Cool!"

Before Aaron could say anything else, Mr. Dante stepped back up on the podium. I glanced at Natasha; her cheeks were pink. I hoped mine weren't.

Last semester, I'd had a pretty big crush on Aaron, and Natasha knew it. And now she was kind of dating him. Which was totally fine with me—I'd actually helped set them up, because I knew they liked each other. But being in an ensemble with my friend's almost-boyfriend who I used to like (and was sort of still getting over) . . . yeah, that could be a little bit awkward.

Maybe that was another part of making it halfway through middle school. *Congratulations! All your friendships are about to get twice as complicated.*

𝄞

Lunch was now total proof of that. It used to be pretty simple—me, Julia, and Natasha at our regular table. But now, lunch involved boys.

Specifically, Seth Anderson—Julia's boyfriend. Not almost-boyfriend, like Natasha and Aaron. *Boyfriend* boyfriend. So he ate lunch with us. Which was totally cool, don't get me wrong—I liked Seth a lot. He played cello in the school orchestra, he was really into photography, and when he found out about my obsession with horror movies, he let me borrow his book of Edgar Allan Poe stories (which was *amazing*, and had some pretty wicked illustrations, too).

Still, lunch was different once he started eating with us. Because Julia was different.

"That test in Spanish yesterday was really hard," Natasha said as we left the cubby room. I nodded in agreement.

"Mr. Hernandez is losing it, I swear." I held the band-hall door open for her and Julia, and we headed to the cafeteria together. "I didn't recognize half of those vocabulary words."

"That's what Seth said," Julia chimed in. "He has Mr. Hernandez seventh period."

"Hey, I forgot to tell you!" Natasha said suddenly, nudging me. "We ordered Lotus Garden last night for dinner, and Chad delivered it! My dad gave him a five-dollar tip, and I said that would cover half a load of laundry. He looked pretty mad."

Julia and I laughed. Not only was my brother pretty much the messiest human being on the planet, he refused to learn how to operate a washing machine. At ten bucks a load, I was making decent money keeping his clothes clean—although sometimes I wondered if it was worth it. I mean, doing his laundry meant dealing with underwear. Which was why I wore rubber gloves.

"I might up my price," I told them. "Last weekend he played football for, like, six straight hours. Oh my God, that load of clothes—I almost passed out from the smell, I swear."

"Still, the extra money must be nice," Julia said.

"Seth's been doing yard work for his neighbors, but I bet you make more doing your brother's laundry. Oh, did I tell you guys I met Seth's sister over the break? She's a music major! She plays piano, but she's a singer, too, and . . ."

Julia kept talking, and Natasha and I shared an amused look. Amused, and maybe a little exasperated, too. Lately it seemed like it was pretty much impossible to talk about anything without Julia bringing up Seth.

That was probably why we only spent half our lunch period together lately. I mean, it wasn't *just* because of Julia. Aaron had lunch then, too, and Natasha usually went and sat with him after she finished eating. She'd been worried about leaving me at first—and honestly, it might have bothered me if I'd been stuck as a third wheel with Julia and Seth. But I had someone else I could sit with, too.

"See you in seventh?" I asked Julia, standing and crumpling my lunch bag. Natasha was on her feet, too, brushing the crumbs off her skirt.

Julia nodded. "Tell Owen I said hi."

I glanced at her, because she sounded like she was trying not to laugh. "What?"

"What?" Julia asked innocently. "Nothing!"

"She thinks you like Owen," Seth told me. Julia smacked his arm, and Natasha giggled.

I rolled my eyes. Right before winter break, I'd asked my friend Owen Reynolds to the spring dance. For whatever reason, Julia and Natasha both found that funny. No matter how many times I told them it wasn't a *date* date.

"I do like Owen." I smiled at Seth. "That's why we're friends."

Julia nodded in agreement. "For now."

Natasha walked to the trash cans with me, still grinning. "She's just giving you a hard time."

"I know." I tossed my bag in the garbage. "Kind of weird that she talked about me and Owen with Seth, though."

"Well," Natasha pointed out, "she can't talk to Seth about *Seth*."

I snickered. "True." And honestly, I was kind of flattered. Julia had spent so much time lately talking about her boyfriend, I'd been wondering if she was even interested in the rest of us anymore.

Natasha headed off to Aaron's table. Most of his friends were in eighth grade, like him. I didn't really know any of them, but Natasha said they were pretty nice. She didn't talk about them much. Actually, she didn't even talk about Aaron much, and not just in comparison to Julia.

I plunked down next to Owen, who was shuffling a stack of Warlock game cards. "I'm in!"

"Good timing," Owen said, smiling. He handed me half of his stack. Across the table, Trevor Wells sighed.

"You know the reason you keep losing is because you split your cards with her," he informed Owen. "Last week she got your draught of death card."

Owen shrugged, brushing the blond hair out of his eyes. "So?"

"So, you would've won if you'd had it."

"Come on, Trevor." I flipped through my stack and glanced at the goblin-chief card he'd tossed in the center of the table. "It's not about winning and losing, it's about having fun. And freezing your goblin chief with my ice sword is really, really fun."

I placed my card on top of Trevor's with a flourish, and everyone laughed. Everyone except Trevor, of course. He was always a sore loser.

"Everyone" was Owen, Max Foster (who played trombone in advanced band, like Trevor), and Brent McEwan and Erin Peale from fifth-period science. And today there was a new guy who I vaguely recognized from my history class last year. Keith or Kyle or something like that.

Ten minutes later, Max was pretty much destroying all of us, which was nothing new. (Although Owen and I really would have had a better chance if we'd each had a full deck of cards.) I'd managed to snag one of Trevor's undead-warrior cards, along with the goblin chief. When Max scored his shield cloak, Trevor threw his cards down in frustration and started arguing with him.

"Guess that's the end of that game." I handed Owen back his cards.

"The bell's about to ring, anyway," he said, wrapping a rubber band around the deck and tucking it into his backpack. Out of habit, I glanced over at Aaron's table.

They were all laughing at something—all except for Natasha. She was smiling, though. I squinted, trying to read her expression. It might have been my imagination, but sometimes I thought Natasha looked a little uncomfortable sitting with Aaron's friends.

"You okay?" Owen asked.

"What?" I glanced at him, startled, and realized he'd seen me staring. And since Owen knew I liked—*used* to like—Aaron, that's probably who he thought I was staring at. "No! I mean, yeah. I'm okay." My face felt a little warm, so I ducked down to pick up my backpack. "Do you have our proposal for Mrs. Driscoll?"

"Yup."

"What are you guys doing for the science fair?" Erin asked, and Owen immediately launched into a detailed description of our project. I was pretty excited about it, too, actually—I mean, it was about aliens on Mars, how could that not be cool? Right now I was too distracted to think about it, though. The science fair wasn't until May, and I had to focus on all-region band, where I'd be performing with a bunch of kids from other middle schools. And we'd only have two rehearsals to learn the music. Then there was the contest on the band trip to worry about, plus my solo for Solo and Ensemble. Oh, and now I was supposed to learn this crazy-hard music for a trio with my former crush who was now kinda dating one of my best friends.

My other classes might have gotten more intense, but band was officially *insane*.

"We could just pick a different planet."

My thumbs flew over my game controller. "Nah," I said without taking my eyes off the TV screen. "If Mrs. Driscoll's right and four of last year's science fair projects were about alien life on Mars, making ours Venus or something won't make our project stand out enough."

"True," Owen admitted. Thursdays after school were our designated hangout time. And after spending the last hour and a half working on our science fair proposal, a little *Prophet Wars* was definitely in order.

Owen jabbed at his controller, and my side of the screen went black. "Sorry," he said with a little grin.

I sighed. "That never would've happened if I had my tank."

"You mean *my* tank." Owen laughed when I scowled at him. "Hey, I won it fair and square, right?"

"Right," I muttered. Over winter break, Owen and I

had watched his favorite movie, *Cyborgs versus Ninjas*. We had a bet that I couldn't guess who the bad guys were halfway through. I'd been positive I was going to win—I could guess the ending to pretty much any movie that wasn't horror, because they were always so predictable.

Cyborgs versus Ninjas was the first time I'd ever been wrong. I was still kind of annoyed about it, although the movie actually *had* been pretty good. But hello, how was I supposed to know the cyborgs were being controlled by evil aliens? And losing the bet meant I had to give Owen my *Prophets* character's tank.

Worf, Owen's dog, whimpered at my feet. I leaned over to scratch him behind the ears until my character reappeared. Soon she was wearing a giant gas mask and hacking her way through a jungle of red vines.

"You know," I realized out loud, "Mrs. Driscoll said there's been a lot of science fair projects on what humans would need to survive on an alien planet. But what if we did one on what aliens would need to live on Earth?"

"You mean like if they built a colony here?" Owen asked, blowing up a pod and sending my character flying. She landed in a puddle of glowing greenish stuff.

"Yeah, like an alien habitat or something. Thanks for the nuclear armor, by the way." My character was sprinting through the vines now, which melted as soon as she touched them.

"An alien habitat," Owen repeated. "And then

people could visit it to see how they lived."

I laughed. "Sounds like *Jurassic Park,* but with aliens instead of dinosaurs. Hey!"

My character had frozen mid-leap. Owen stared at me, his thumb still on the pause button.

"Alien Park!" he said excitedly. "That could be our project—a theme park with aliens from Mars!"

I stared back at him. "That . . . would be *awesome*."

Owen dropped his controller and grabbed the folder with our science fair proposal off the coffee table.

"We could still use a lot of this," he said, flipping through our notes. "Like all this stuff about what an alien's respiratory system would have to be like to live on Mars, and what kind of food they'd eat. But there's a lot we'd have to change, too."

"Mrs. Driscoll said we had to have our proposals revised by Tuesday," I said. "Want to work on it Monday after school?"

"Yes," Owen said immediately, then groaned. "Oh. No, I can't."

"Why not?"

He made a face. "Baseball tryouts."

I patted my knee, and Worf jumped up into my lap. "*Oof,* he's getting too big for this," I said. "Anyway, I thought baseball tryouts were last Monday. That's what Aaron said."

"That was for the eighth-grade team." Owen sounded glum. "Next Monday's for seventh-graders."

"Ah." I cleared my throat. "So . . . you're trying out?"

"Yeah."

"Owen, you hate baseball."

"Yeah."

Scratching Worf behind the ears, I watched as Owen started adding notes to our proposal. "You know, you don't have to try out just because Steve wants you to play."

Steve was Owen's stepdad. He was nice and all, but he *really* wanted Owen to like sports as much as he did. And he never seemed to notice what an amazing artist Owen was. Seriously, the boy could draw flame-spitting dragons and armor-clad trolls good enough to hang in a museum.

Owen shrugged without looking up. "It's not a big deal. I probably won't make it, anyway."

That's not the point, I wanted to say. "Okay."

"What about tomorrow before school?" he asked. "We could meet in Mrs. Driscoll's room—she'll be there for tutoring. I could see if my mom can drop me off early."

Now it was my turn to make a face. "Can't. I'm supposed to work on that trio with Aaron and Liam. Ugh."

Owen glanced at me. "What's wrong?"

"It's insanely hard," I told him. "And Solo and Ensemble is less than a month away. *And* I found out they were both in an ensemble together last year that did really well, but this is my first one and if I mess up, then all three of us will get a bad rating and—"

"Holly, you can do it," Owen interrupted. "That's why Mr. Dante put you three in an ensemble together. You're all first chair in your sections—he knows you can handle it."

"I guess so." I smiled as he went back to jotting down notes. Every time I got nervous about something, like chair tests or science quizzes, Owen always managed to make me feel better. I wished he had that kind of confidence in himself.

𝄞

By the time I got to the band hall before school on Friday, the butterflies were back in full force. I grabbed my horn and hurried to a practice room, hoping to play through "Triptych" at least once before Aaron and Liam showed up. I'd practiced it last night for almost an hour. (It would've been a whole hour if Chad hadn't started kicking the wall our rooms shared until I stopped.)

I played it once, then twice, and was almost through it a third time when the practice-room door opened.

"Sorry we're late," Aaron said with an apologetic smile.

"It's okay!" I watched him drop his backpack on his chair, then stand back to let Liam in. With the three of us plus Liam's tuba, the practice room suddenly felt kind of cramped.

"Hi, Holly." Liam sat down, carefully balancing the tuba on his knees and opening his music folder.

"Hi." I toyed nervously with the red-and-purple

beaded bracelet on my wrist. Julia had made it as a Christmas present, along with a pair of really cool earrings for Natasha. "So . . . have you guys played through this at all yet?"

"Yeah, sort of." Liam stifled a yawn.

"I haven't really looked at it," Aaron said. His brow furrowed as he dug through his travesty of a backpack. Seriously, Aaron was extremely nice and extremely cute, but he was the most unorganized person *ever*. (Well, except for Chad.)

My fingers twitched when several crumpled balls of paper fell from Aaron's bag, followed by a few pens and a broken protractor. Really, how hard is it to actually use folders and a pencil bag?

"Here it is." Aaron pulled out a small square of paper and unfolded it. I saw the title "Triptych" at the top and cringed—it was so wrinkled, I couldn't even see how Aaron was going to read the notes. And when he started cramming all the pens and other junk back into his backpack, I practically had to sit on my hands to keep myself from flattening out all his papers and making good use of the mostly empty binder sticking out of the bag.

Setting the music on his stand, Aaron squinted. "Yeah, this looks kind of hard. What's your part like?" He leaned over until his shoulder was pretty much touching mine. "Wow, that looks crazy, too."

He sat up straight again, which made me feel equal parts relieved and disappointed, followed by a healthy dose of guilt. *He's Natasha's boyfriend*, I told the butterflies in my stomach firmly. *Get over it already.*

"Harder than that quartet we were in last year," Liam agreed. "'Schizo.'"

"'Scherzo,'" Aaron corrected him with a grin.

"That's what I said."

"This is harder than that was, really?" I couldn't keep the worry out of my voice. "So you guys think we can learn this by next month?"

"Yeah, sure," Aaron said. "It's not *that* bad."

I looked at my music, then arched an eyebrow at him. Aaron laughed.

"Okay, it's hard," he said. "But it's pretty short. I mean, compared to our other band music."

Well, that was true.

"Should we just try the first eight bars?" Liam asked, and I nodded.

"Okay."

"All right." Aaron started tapping his foot in a slow, steady beat, then counted us off. "One, two, three, four . . ."

We played. And it . . . wasn't bad. Not good, but not catastrophic, either. By the time we finished, I was already feeling a little bit better. Okay, maybe I was picturing where I'd put the medal you get for a Superior rating on a solo or ensemble in my room. Probably on my bulletin board. Or maybe on my bookshelf. And hey, if I did well on my solo, I'd have *two* medals.

"Should we try up to measure sixteen?" Aaron was

saying, and I blinked. Time to stop daydreaming about medals and actually rehearse.

After half an hour, we could pretty much play the first half of "Triptych" without stopping or making too many mistakes. I mean, we were playing it pretty slow, but still.

"This isn't so bad," Liam said, emptying his spit valve. "The first time we rehearsed our quartet last year, I kept getting lost."

"Yeah, so did I." Aaron smiled at me. "You sound great, Holly," he added. "I promise I'll practice more before next week."

"What? No!" I sputtered, feeling my face grow warm. "You don't have to practice . . . I mean, you should, because—no, I mean you sound great, too!"

For the love . . . *stop talking, Holly.*

Liam yawned hugely. "No chance we can do this after school next time?" he asked Aaron. "I kind of hate mornings."

"Sorry," Aaron replied. "Baseball." The first bell rang, and we started packing up. I tried not to watch as Aaron stuffed his copy of "Triptych" back in his bag. Seriously, did the boy not have a music folder? Oh wait, it was probably lost in the chaos that was his cubby.

"Hey, you have the third *Watch the Fog* movie on DVD, right?" Aaron asked me.

"Yeah, although I think my brother loaned it to one of his friends," I answered, stacking my music neatly and sliding it into my folder. (Yes, I was trying to set a good example in the hopes that my neatness would inspire him. A girl could dream.) "I can check if you want to borrow it, though."

"That'd be great!" Aaron said. "Hey, I finally saw *House of the Wicked*. You were right, it was awesome."

I nodded. "Definitely one of my all-time favorites. And the sequel comes out in a few months!"

The three of us talked about horror movies while we put our instruments up and left the band hall (although I couldn't understand half of what Liam said because he kept yawning). When we rounded the corner and I saw Julia at her locker with Seth and Natasha, my stomach tightened.

You aren't doing anything wrong, I told myself. And Natasha didn't look upset to see us walking together. Still, I made sure to keep a safe distance from Aaron, just in case.

I waved to Liam when he headed down the hall to his locker, then joined Julia and Seth while Natasha talked to Aaron. (His locker was right next to Julia's.)

"How'd the trio stuff go?" Julia's voice was light, but she was looking at me intently. I glanced over my shoulder at Aaron, then gave Julia a reassuring smile.

"It's hard, but not as hard as I thought it would be."

I meant it, too. "Triptych" wasn't so bad. Neither was being in a trio with Aaron. In fact, I was happy to be in an ensemble with a friend. And the sooner the butterflies in my stomach realized that's all he was, the happier I'd be.

Chapter Three

I spent most of the weekend helping my parents *finally* take down all our Christmas decorations. (Seriously, the tree was looking pathetic. Half the pine needles had fallen off—walking near it in bare feet was just asking for trouble.) While Chad was out with his friends, I snuck in a lot of good practice time on my horn solo, which was hard but also really fun to play. There was a piano part, too, but I wouldn't get to rehearse it with Mrs. Benitez, the choir director who accompanied pretty much everyone's solo, until right before Solo and Ensemble Competition. Yet another thing to worry about—what if I messed up because I wasn't used to hearing the piano part? I decided to memorize my solo, just in case. That way, hopefully, I wouldn't get lost, no matter what it sounded like with piano.

Owen told me in science on Monday that he'd spent his weekend at the batting cages with Steve, practicing for baseball tryouts. So Monday night I rewrote our proposal for the science fair project myself. I even made a cover page that said *Alien Park* and had a funny image of aliens riding a roller coaster that I found online. It wasn't nearly as cool as Owen's sketches, but I was pretty happy with it overall.

When I got to science on Tuesday, Owen was already at his desk, sketchbook out, drawing furiously. Even from the door, I could tell from his expression that he was upset about something.

I set my backpack down on the desk next to his and glanced at the sketch. My eyes widened a little. No dragons or trolls this time—he was drawing himself in a baseball uniform. A speeding baseball had apparently smacked him in the chest, and he was falling backward, the bat flying out of his hands. It kind of looked like the time Trevor had gotten hit with a volleyball during our bake-sale fund-raiser last semester and fell right on our table of brownies and cupcakes. Except in the drawing, Owen was about to fall onto a pile of baseball gloves, which—I leaned forward, squinting—had really long, wicked nails, like evil glove-claws. Yikes.

"So I guess baseball tryouts didn't go too well?" I asked, sitting at my desk.

Owen looked surprised to see me. "Oh, hey." He glanced back down at his drawing. "No, they went fine. I made the JV team, actually."

"What? How?" I clapped my hand over my mouth, hoping I hadn't hurt his feelings. "I mean, congratulations!"

With a halfhearted smile, Owen closed his sketchbook. "Thanks, but it's just second string. I probably won't play much." He made a face. "And now I've got practice after school, plus all the games. Including Thursdays," he added.

"Oh." I chewed my lip. "Well, that's okay. I've got all-region rehearsal Friday, so I should probably practice after school Thursday, anyway." Owen still looked miserable, and to be honest, I was pretty bummed at the thought of not getting any *Prophets* time with him for the next month or so, too. "I guess Steve was pretty happy about it, huh?" I asked, trying to sound cheerful.

Owen shrugged. "Yeah. My mom, too. Anyway . . . do you have our proposal?"

"Yup!" I pulled the packet out of my bag and handed it to Owen. His face brightened when he saw the cover page.

"Nice!"

"Thanks."

"I'm really sorry I didn't help more," he added, flipping through the pages.

"Don't worry about it." I glanced at his sketchbook. Something was sticking out—it looked like a page from a magazine. "Hey, what's that?"

"What?" Owen looked down. "Oh, nothing."

He pushed the page back inside the sketchbook, but I'd already seen the title.

"That was for an art contest?" I asked excitedly. "What kind?"

Owen's face was a little red. "It's just this drawing competition. The winners get to go to an animation workshop in San Antonio for a weekend."

"Awesome!" I exclaimed. "Are you entering? You are, right?"

"No. I don't know . . . maybe."

"Owen, you *have* to," I said firmly, and he blushed even more. "No, seriously. Promise you'll enter."

He smiled down at his sketchbook. "Okay, I promise."

If ten bucks per load was a fair price for doing my brother's laundry, then I'd have to charge at least a hundred to clean out his car. It wasn't even a car anymore. It was a giant garbage can with wheels and an engine.

I sat in the passenger seat Friday morning, knees pulled up to my chest so I wouldn't get grease on my shoes from all the mostly empty Lotus Garden cartons. Chad took a sharp turn, and soda sloshed out of the cup holder and onto my horn case.

"Ew," I muttered, wiping my case with a napkin that wasn't all that clean to begin with. "I cannot believe Mom had a meeting this morning."

"That's the thanks I get for hauling you all the way across town." Chad started flipping through radio stations while we sat at a red light. "You're welcome, by the way."

"Yeah, thanks a lot for driving me around in the trash mobile."

"I don't get why you've got this band thing at Bishop High School, anyway," Chad said. "Everyone from Millican goes to Ridgewood."

I sighed. "It's all-*region* band, Chad. Kids from all over the *region*. The concert's always at a high school, and this year it's Bishop's turn to host."

Just saying it out loud—*all-region band*—made me wish I hadn't forced down that bowl of cereal before we left. The whole thing was kind of insane—rehearse today and tomorrow, then perform at a concert tomorrow night? What if it sounded horrible? The music wasn't that hard, but still . . .

I hopped out of Chad's car with my horn case and my folder, unstuck a napkin from my shoe, and tossed the two cans that had fallen out back onto the seat.

"What, no tip?" Chad asked, holding out his hand. I slapped the sticky napkin into his palm.

"There you go."

I hurried across the lawn away from the entrance. The letter Mr. Dante had given us said there were doors to the band hall on the side of the school, so we wouldn't have to go through the front and wander through the hallways with a bunch of high-schoolers. Sure enough, I saw a set of double doors propped open with two music stands, each with a sign reading WELCOME TO ALL-REGION BAND!

I stepped inside, glancing at my watch. I was pretty early. Okay, I was half an hour early—I totally lied to Chad about what time I needed to be here because I knew we'd be late if I didn't.

There were a few kids milling around, but they mostly looked like high-schoolers. I passed the cubby room and did a double take. It was *huge*. Whoa, and they had vending machines right outside. I grinned, wondering what Gabby would say when she saw them. She'd gotten in trouble last semester because she kept eating candy before band, and all the sugar had a pretty gross effect on her saxophone. Glancing around at the cubbies, I wondered if any of these instruments had ants in them. Hopefully high-schoolers were better about cleaning their instruments than Gabby.

I headed down the hall past the cubbies, then went through the next set of double doors into the band hall. It was . . . disappointingly small. All-region auditions had been at Ridgewood, and that band hall was way bigger than this. Actually, Bishop's band hall looked about the same size as Millican's. Kind of weird, considering it was a pretty big high school.

A woman in a Bishop Band T-shirt was arranging chairs and music stands in the middle of the room. She glanced up and smiled at me.

"Here for all-region?" she asked.

"Yes," I said nervously. "Is there a seating chart?"

"There will be," she said cheerfully, pointing at a stack of papers on the director's podium. "I'm about to start putting names on chairs so you all know where to sit."

"Do you need help?" I wasn't trying to be such

a kiss-up, I swear. I was just really nervous. Doing anything organizational would help me calm down.

But the woman beamed. "I'd love it!"

We talked while we adjusted stands and set the pages with individual printed names on each chair. Her name was Ms. Hunter, she was the assistant band director at Bishop, and she played the French horn, too. She acted really disappointed when I said I was going to Ridgewood, which made me blush.

"I could always use great horn players," she said with a wink. "Especially ones who know how to show up early."

"I can't stand being late," I said vehemently, making my way down the row where the clarinets would sit. I was about to tell her how I'd lied to Chad when I noticed the name on my next page. JULIA GORDON, MILLICAN.

"Oh, so this is the concert band," I realized out loud. "Where's the symphonic band rehearsing?"

"In the band hall," Ms. Hunter replied.

"This isn't the band hall?" I asked, glancing back at the cubbies. "Is it the choir room or something?"

Ms. Hunter shook her head. "It's our ensemble room." When I stared at her blankly, she grinned. "Like a second band hall."

Whoa.

"Um, where's the band hall?" I asked, setting the last page down.

"Just across the corridor," she said. "So you're in the advanced symphonic band?"

"Yes."

"As a seventh-grader?"

"Yes." I tried to sound modest.

She laughed. "Now I *really* wish you were coming to Bishop."

I liked Ms. Hunter.

By the time we finished setting up, more kids were milling around, and they definitely weren't all high-schoolers. I grabbed my horn case and headed for the band hall—the *other* band hall. (Seriously, how cool was that?)

When I walked in, I froze.

It was *huge*. No, seriously. The Bishop band hall was, like, the size of a football field. Okay, maybe not *that* huge. But it was definitely bigger than the one at Ridgewood, and you could probably fit four or five Millican band halls inside it.

"Holly!"

Relief swooped through me when I spotted Julia, Natasha, and Gabby waving from the corner, and I hurried over to join them.

"Did you just get here?" Julia asked. "I figured you'd be, like, an hour early."

"Half an hour," I told her. "I was in the ensemble room helping the director set up chairs."

"There's an ensemble room?" Natasha asked, and I nodded.

"It's like a *second band hall*," I told her, and her eyes widened. "That's where the concert band is rehearsing."

"That's us!" Julia said, nudging Natasha with her clarinet case. "I guess we should head over there."

After I showed Julia and Natasha where the ensemble room was, Gabby and I found our seats. We were only three chairs apart, which was nice . . . although I wished we were sitting next to each other like we did at Millican. Now that rehearsal was actually about to start, my nerves were back full force. But Gabby never seemed nervous about anything.

I cleaned my mouthpiece about six times while everyone milled around, looking for their names and settling into their seats. Aaron waved to me from his chair down the row behind me, and past him, I saw Liam in the tuba section, looking bleary-eyed. Glancing down at the seat to my left, I just barely had time to read NIKHIL BANSAL, FOREST HILL on the paper before someone plopped a horn case on it. I looked up to see a very cute boy with curly black hair and long eyelashes smiling at me.

"I remember you," he said. "From the volleyball game."

That caught me off guard, and I opened and closed my mouth a few times before saying, "Huh?"

Smooth, Holly.

"Last semester," he went on, opening his case. "You guys were doing a bake sale. The brownies were great."

"Oh!" And suddenly, I *did* remember him from one of the games. We'd talked for a few seconds before some rude girls behind him in line interrupted us. "You said your mom's the volleyball coach at Forest Hill, right?"

"Yeah." He smiled and held his hand out. "I'm Nick, by the way."

"I'm Holly." We shook hands, which felt weirdly formal. I was glad I'd been holding the rag to clean my mouthpiece, though—my hand would've been a lot sweatier otherwise. When Nick sat down, I glanced to my right and saw Gabby waggling her eyebrows at me in this ridiculously exaggerated way, and I struggled not to laugh.

The head band director for Bishop stepped onto the podium, and the few kids still standing took their seats quickly. After he gave us a welcome speech and talked about the concert a little, he introduced our conductor. Her name was Meredith Collier, she used to teach a high-school band in Dallas, and now she was a college music professor.

And suddenly I didn't have time to think about how nervous I was anymore, because rehearsal *flew*. Even tuning, which was normally kind of boring, went by fast with Mrs. Collier. We spent over an hour doing a bunch of different warm-ups, but she was so energetic and funny that it didn't feel long at all. The first piece of music we rehearsed for the concert was a march, and it turned out to be pretty easy. We sight-read through the whole thing without stopping, and when we got to the end, I couldn't help smiling.

Playing in a really, really good band was *fun*.

By the time lunch rolled around, we had the march

down and we'd played through this slow chorale several times. We started on "Lenore Overture," too, which I could already tell was going to be the hardest of all five pieces we were doing. But we still had the rest of the afternoon, plus rehearsal tomorrow. I was feeling a lot more confident about the whole thing.

Nick turned out to be really nice. We even ate lunch together, along with Gabby and two of Nick's friends from Forest Hill, Ian and Rachel. I told them the story about the ants in Gabby's saxophone, and they cracked up. (Then I told Gabby about the vending machines by the ensemble room and she practically sprinted down the hall, which made us laugh even harder.)

Before I knew it, the afternoon rehearsal was over and I was hopping into Dad's (blissfully clean) car. By the time we got home, I'd gone over the entire rehearsal and showed him my all-region shirt, which had everyone's names by section on the back. Then I went over the whole thing again over dinner for Mom and Chad (who put his headphones on after two minutes).

On Saturday, rehearsal didn't start till afternoon. Julia, Natasha, and I made plans to have lunch at Natasha's house, then her dad would drive us to Bishop. But when Natasha opened her front door, I could tell by the look on her face that something was up.

"No, it's totally fine," she said into the phone cradled between her shoulder and ear, motioning for me to come inside. "Yeah, I know! Anyway, Holly's here, so we'll just see you at rehearsal, okay? Okay . . . bye."

Natasha hung up and gave me an exasperated look.

"Julia's not coming," I said, and she nodded. "And I'm guessing it has something to do with Seth."

Natasha shrugged. "Well, it's his birthday today," she told me. "And she can't do anything with him tonight because of the concert, so I guess they're having lunch."

"So why'd she say she'd have lunch with us in the first place?" I asked.

"Because Seth was supposed to go to his grandparents' place today, but I guess his plans changed at the last minute."

"Ah." I tried not to feel annoyed as I followed Natasha into the kitchen. I mean, I completely understood why Julia would want to hang out with Seth on his birthday. Still, being blown off for a guy by your best friend doesn't feel great.

"Hey, Julia's birthday is coming up," I realized out loud while Natasha pulled cold cuts and mustard out of the fridge. "It's the weekend before the band trip, I think."

"Oh, right! What do you think she'll want to do?" Natasha asked.

"Last year we went to the movies." I made a face. "*The Impossible Marriage*, or something."

"*The Impossible* Wedding," Natasha corrected me. "I loved that movie!" She giggled when I made a gagging noise. "Anyway, maybe we should throw Julia a surprise party."

I grabbed a loaf of bread and a stack of napkins. "That would be cool! How about a sleepover?"

Natasha glanced up with a little smile. "Because then it would be girls only?"

"Well . . . yeah," I admitted, adding a slice of cheese to my sandwich. "I like Seth a lot, I really do, but . . ."

"But it's been a while since we've hung out with Julia without him," Natasha finished. "Yeah, I know."

"Plus, we haven't had a sleepover in forever," I went on. "And that way Julia can spend the day with Seth, and we can decorate the living room and make a cake and all that. I'll invite her over for dinner, but I can tell her mom so she can secretly pack her overnight stuff . . ."

"So it'll actually be a surprise!" Natasha grinned. "This'll be fun."

"Yeah." I took a bite of sandwich, pleased. "Maybe we can rent some movies."

"Movies Julia would like," Natasha said quickly. "Not one of your freaky movies with people crawling on the ceiling and stuff."

My eyes widened in surprise. "Hey, you saw the sequel to *Watch the Fog*?"

"I watched it with Aaron." Natasha shook her head. "Correction—I watched half of it with Aaron. I spent the other half talking to his mom in the kitchen."

I laughed. "You just left him watching it alone?"

"Nah, some of his friends were over, too." Natasha was focused on cutting her sandwich into pieces with a knife and fork. I watched her for a few seconds.

"I've always wondered why you do that," I said at last, and she glanced up.

"What?"

"Cut your sandwich up."

"Oh." She smiled. "You'll think I'm stupid, but I swear it tastes better bite-size. And before you say anything," she added when I started laughing, "remember the Halloween candy."

"What?"

Natasha gave me a pointed look. "At Halloween, you made your mom buy, like, ten bags of those mini Snickers and Three Musketeers because you said . . . ?"

She waited expectantly, and I sighed. "Because they taste better than the regular-size ones. But that's different!"

"So not different." Natasha popped a piece of turkey sandwich into her mouth and grinned.

"If you say so." I chewed slowly, trying to think of how to ask my next question without sounding too nosy. "So . . . are Aaron's friends nice?"

"Sure! They're okay," said Natasha. "Why?"

"Just curious." I grabbed a glass from the cabinet and filled it with water. "I don't really know any of them. Like the ones you sit with at lunch."

"Yeah, they're all in eighth grade." Natasha pushed the last piece of sandwich around her plate. "Some guys he was on the football team with. A few of the girls are cheerleaders. One's on the debate team, too."

I waited, because it sounded like she wanted to say more.

"I guess we just don't have a lot in common," she said at last. "Me and his friends. You know? They're nice and everything, but . . . I don't know." She laughed self-consciously. "It's not a big deal. I guess I'm not like Julia, the way she wants to be around Seth all the time. I mean, I really like Aaron! But that doesn't mean I have to spend every second with him. Is that . . . weird?"

I smiled. "No, I don't think it's weird at all."

Natasha looked relieved. "Thanks." After a moment, she grinned. "Looks like you're always having fun with Owen at lunch, though."

"Yeah, I do." I shook my head when she waggled her eyebrows in a way that reminded me of Gabby. "Why are you and Julia so obsessed with this Owen thing? You do know that if I actually *did* have a crush on him, I'd tell you guys, right?"

Natasha laughed. "Yeah, I know you would. We mostly just do it to annoy you. And . . ."

"And?" I prompted.

"And maybe we really do think you'd be cute together."

I rolled my eyes, but Mr. Prynne saved me from responding when he called us from the living room.

"You girls about ready to go?"

"Just a sec!" Natasha and I cleaned off the table, then double-checked to make sure we had everything—horns, music, plus the dress clothes we'd need for the concert. We spent most of the drive planning Julia's surprise party, and before I knew it, Mr. Prynne was dropping us off at Bishop. I spotted Nick with a few of his friends from Forest Hill across the band hall. He waved, and I waved back.

"Who's that?" Natasha asked immediately.

"Nick. He plays French horn, too," I told her. "We sit next to each other."

"I remember him!" she exclaimed, still peering across the band hall. "From the volleyball game, right?"

"Yeah, that was him."

"He's really cute!" Natasha looked like she wanted to say something else, but Aaron had just walked in. "I'm going to go say hi before rehearsal," she told me. "See you at the concert, okay?"

"Okay!"

Rehearsal was just as fun as yesterday. We spent a few hours just on "Lenore Overture," and by the end of rehearsal, it was my favorite song out of the five pieces we'd be performing. It was hard, but when we played it all the way through, it sounded seriously impressive.

The Bishop band boosters had dinner set up for us in the cafeteria. I piled spaghetti and salad onto my plate while Gabby went straight to the dessert table and loaded up on an obscene amount of cookies. We stood together at the end of the table, scanning the crowd.

"There's Natasha and Aaron," Gabby said, and I saw them with Liam and a few other kids from Millican. Natasha caught my eye and pointed, and I saw Julia leaning against the wall near the entrance, talking on her cell phone. To Seth, no doubt. I sighed, and Natasha shrugged.

"Want to go sit with them?" Gabby asked around a mouthful of cookie. Then her eyes flickered to something behind me, and she grinned.

"What?" I turned to see Nick waving me over to his table.

"Go over there!" Gabby gave me a little push, and I held my plate steady.

"Come with me," I said, and she rolled her eyes.

"Chicken."

"Oh, come on." I looked pointedly at his table. "It's not like that—he's sitting with Ian and Rachel, like lunch yesterday."

"Whatever you say." Gabby followed me to Nick's table, and I said a silent prayer she wouldn't do anything crazy. Gabby was a great friend, but pretty much nothing seemed to embarrass her, and the way she smiled at me anytime Nick was around made me nervous.

But it turned out I had nothing to worry about. We just swapped band stories with Nick and his friends, and talked about our band trips. And before I knew it, dinner was over and we were getting ready for the concert.

I slipped into the back of the auditorium right before the concert band's performance and spotted my parents and Chad near the middle. But I stayed near the back, since I'd have to leave before the last song to go warm up.

It was hard to see Natasha, but Julia was right on the end of the row of clarinets. She was wearing a new dress, one I'd never seen before. And I knew it was kind of silly, but it made me feel sad. I saw Julia every day, but we just didn't get to talk as much about this kind of stuff anymore. Not that a new dress was all that important, but she hadn't even mentioned buying it or anything.

The concert band sounded great. Like, *really* great. By the time I got back to the band hall, I was excited about our performance. Mrs. Collier led us through our warm-ups, then we filed down the corridor. My stomach fluttered when I walked onto the stage—I hadn't really noticed before, but the auditorium was *packed*.

While Mrs. Collier talked to the audience, Nick leaned over.

"Are your parents here?" he asked.

"Yeah, and my brother. Yours?"

"Yup," he replied. "My brother, too, because he owes me. I've been to every play and musical he's done this year."

"Is he in high school?"

"Nope, eighth grade," Nick told me. "We're twins."

"Oh, cool." I glanced out into the crowd again. "My brother's a junior. My parents make me go to his games sometimes. A musical sounds like more fun, at least."

"You wouldn't say that if you had to live with him,"

Nick said wryly. "Last year he was in *Beauty and the Beast*. He made me read lines with him. By the end, I had the whole part memorized. All the songs, too."

I glanced at him. "Wait, what part did he play?"

"The Beast." Nick grinned when I stifled a giggle. "Yeah, he made me learn Belle's lines. I was pretty good, if I do say so myself." He sighed. "Dancing with him was sort of awkward, though."

I was still laughing when Mrs. Collier stepped up onto the podium, which was good because I pretty much forgot to be nervous. And just like rehearsal, the concert flew by. Before I knew it, we were starting "Lenore Overture," our last piece . . . which sounded amazing. Maybe it was just my imagination, but something about being onstage in the enormous auditorium made us sound almost professional. When we finished, I had goose bumps all over my arms.

Mrs. Collier had us stand to take a bow while the audience applauded. I couldn't help but think that it was kind of funny how much time I'd spent practicing the all-region audition music, and how quickly the whole thing was over. Everyone started packing up as the lights came back up over the crowd. A few kids were already making their way offstage to find their friends and family.

"That was fun," Nick said as we put our music back in our folders, and I nodded in agreement. "Hey, Holly?"

"Yeah?"

"Would it be okay if I called you sometime?"

I almost dropped my folder. "Oh!" I stopped myself just in time from asking *why*? "Yeah, I'd . . . um . . . yes. Definitely." Then I stood there and we stared at each other for a second before he said:

"I don't know your phone number."

"Oh! Sorry." Oh my God, seriously. I was really bad at this. But he'd totally caught me off guard—I'd never had a boy ask if he could call me before. Pulling the pencil out of my folder, I grabbed his music and scribbled my phone number at the top of his copy of "Lenore Overture."

"Here you go."

"Thanks!" Nick smiled at me, then glanced around the auditorium. "Well, I guess I should go find my parents."

"Yeah, me too." I tucked the pencil back in my folder, hoping my face wasn't as red as it felt.

"See you!" With a last grin, Nick waved then headed across the stage. The second he started down the stairs, someone socked me on the shoulder.

"Ow!" I turned to find Gabby behind me, her eyes comically wide.

"Did I just see what I think I saw?" she demanded, and I did my best to look innocent. Which was hard, because between our band's awesome performance and what had just happened with Nick, I was feeling all flushed and giddy.

"What are you talking about?"

Gabby arched an eyebrow. "I'm talking about the

fact that I'm ninety-nine percent sure I just saw you give Nick your phone number."

"Oh, that." I started walking to the stairs, Gabby right on my heels.

"Well?" she demanded.

"Well what?"

She made a loud, exasperated noise. "Holly!"

"Okay, okay!" I lowered my voice as a few kids passed us. "He asked if he could call me, so I—"

"Freaking *awesome*!" Gabby yelled before I could finish. I tried to shush her, which was hard because I couldn't stop laughing. "Let's go tell Julia." She pulled me down the stairs, but I tugged my arm away.

"My parents are right there," I told her, pointing to where Mom and Dad were waving. Chad was still in his seat, and I wondered if he'd fallen asleep. Then I noticed Dad's video camera and grinned. I could watch our whole performance as soon as we got home! And again tomorrow. Who was I kidding—I'd probably watch it a dozen times before Monday. "I'll tell Julia about Nick later, okay?" I said, suddenly itching to find out if "Lenore Overture" really sounded as amazing as I thought.

Gabby made a face. "Okay, okay. I guess I should find my mom, too." She dug a package of peanut butter cups out of her pocket and ripped it open. "Gotta eat the evidence first," she said, and I laughed. Gabby's mom was a huge health nut, which was why Gabby ate pretty much nothing but sugary stuff when she wasn't at home.

She offered me one of the peanut butter cups, then held hers up like she was making a toast. "To all-region band . . . a great place to meet boys."

I shook my head, laughing, and we clinked our peanut butter cups together like glasses.

Chapter Five

The next two weeks were a blur. All-region might have been over, but between Solo and Ensemble and the band trip coming up, plus an increasingly ridiculous amount of homework, I felt busier than ever. And it didn't help that me and Owen's *Prophets*-playing days were temporarily over thanks to his baseball practices after school. Blowing up alien pods really would've helped me manage my stress levels. We'd split up the work on our science fair project, but working on it together had been a lot more fun.

Honestly, I just really missed hanging out with him. Maybe more than I'd admit to Julia or Natasha.

At least the trio was coming along okay. Actually, rehearsing with Aaron and Liam was pretty fun. And a few days before Solo and Ensemble, we played "Triptych" all the way through for Mr. Dante. He helped us with a few of the harder spots, but overall, we sounded pretty good. Apparently Mr. Dante thought so, too.

"I'd like you three to perform this on the band trip," he told us. "We have enough time for a few ensembles to play in addition to our three songs. It'd be nice for someone other than the Solo and Ensemble judges to hear this, right?"

"Cool!" said Aaron, and I nodded enthusiastically. Liam yawned, but he looked interested, too.

Since Mr. Dante seemed so confident about the trio, I wasn't too nervous about our performance. My solo was a different story, though. I had it memorized and could play it backward and forward, but Thursday after school was the first time I'd try a run-through with Mrs. Benitez accompanying me.

Nervously, I watched her arrange her sheet music on the piano. "Ready?" she asked with a smile, and I nodded. Through the window to his office, I saw Mr. Dante get up from the computer and stand in the doorway to watch. *There'll be a judge on Saturday,* I reminded myself. *This is a good dress rehearsal.*

"Pastorale for Horn" started with four measures of piano. After about a minute of playing, I relaxed. The piano didn't mess me up—it *helped*. Mrs. Benitez harmonized the melody in the horn part, and hearing all the chords while I played really helped me stay in tune. When we finished, Mr. Dante was smiling.

"I'll have to find a more challenging solo for you next year," he said, and I blushed.

After I packed up my horn, I met Natasha outside of the band hall and we walked to the baseball field together. Owen's first baseball game was today, and even though he said he'd probably spend the whole time on the bench, I wanted to go. Since Aaron was on the varsity team and their game was right after the JV team's, Natasha had decided to come with me. I'd asked Julia during seventh-period computer lab if she wanted to come, but she had a history test tomorrow and her parents had put her on some sort of study lockdown. No phone calls or anything.

"She's not failing again, is she?" I asked Natasha. They were in the same history class.

Natasha shook her head. "No, but she got a C on the last quiz. Apparently, her parents weren't too happy about it."

"Oh." I frowned. "I hope they're still okay with her surprise party."

"I'm sure they will be!"

I spotted Owen's family in the bleachers right away. They were kind of hard to miss in their bright red Millican baseball jerseys. Owen's five-year-old stepsister, Megan, even had a little Millican flag, which she waved frantically as Natasha and I climbed the steps to join them.

"C'mon, I've seen better swings on a porch!" Megan hollered. I glanced down at the field, but the game hadn't even started yet. Sighing, Steve leaned down and turned Megan to face him.

"We've been over this, sweetie," he said seriously. "I know you hear Daddy yell those things when he watches baseball on TV, but you can't yell them here. Okay?"

"Okay." Megan slumped down in her seat, but her face brightened when I sat next to her. "Hi, Holly!"

"Hi," I said with a grin. "Nice flag."

"I feel like we haven't seen you in ages." Mrs. Grady smiled at me. "How are you?"

"Good, thanks." I introduced Natasha to Owen's family right as the players started walking out onto the field. Megan shot to her feet.

"*Owen! Ohhhhhhhhwen!*" she yelled, her flag a red blur. Natasha and I giggled, and Mrs. Grady shook her head.

"She's a little excited," she said, ruffling Megan's hair fondly.

But I could tell she and Steve were excited, too. In fact, the only person who didn't look excited was Owen. He spent the first four innings on the bench, watching the game with a glum expression. I wondered if he was wishing he'd brought his sketchbook.

Natasha leaned closer to me. "Doesn't really look like he's having fun," she whispered. I nodded in agreement, glancing at Owen's parents. They didn't seem to notice at all. And when Owen finally did get up to bat in the fifth inning, they whistled and cheered like crazy. I cheered, too, but I couldn't help picturing that sketch Owen had drawn of the baseball glove-claws. Between that image and the way his shoulders slumped while he walked to the plate, I felt like I was watching him head to the guillotine.

When the pitcher wound up to throw, I winced in anticipation. Owen swung and missed, and I breathed a sigh of relief. At least the ball hadn't knocked him over.

We kept cheering even after he struck out and went back to the bench. But I couldn't help sneaking glances at Owen's parents. It was nice that they were so supportive, but couldn't they tell Owen was miserable?

When the game finally ended, Natasha stood and stretched. "If we're staying for another game, I'm definitely going to need nachos," she told me as we followed the Gradys under the bleachers.

"Get me some, too!" I handed her a few bills, and she headed to the concession stand while I joined Owen and his family outside the locker rooms.

"Really good effort," Steve was saying. "Maybe we'll head back to the batting cages tomorrow after school to work on your swing."

"Tomorrow? I can't, I . . ." Blinking furiously, Owen shot me a pleading look. "We have plans to work on our science project tomorrow. Right, Holly?"

"Um, right." I nodded and tried to smile at Steve. But as soon as the Gradys started heading to their car, I tugged Owen's arm to hold him back. "Um, Owen?"

"I'm sorry," he said immediately. "But there's no practice after school tomorrow, and I really don't want to spend it at the batting cages. Besides, we should probably compare notes on our project. I mean, if you really can come over."

"I can, but Owen—why don't you just tell your parents the truth?" I asked. "They won't be mad if you just say you don't like baseball."

Owen sighed. "I know they won't be *mad*. But they'll be disappointed."

I opened my mouth to argue, then glanced at his family in their matching red jerseys. Megan was still waving her flag as Mrs. Grady buckled her into the backseat of their car.

"Okay, so maybe they'll be disappointed," I admitted. "Still . . . what are you going to do, just pretend to like baseball all through eighth grade, and then high school? That's another *five years* of baseball, Owen."

He made such a sour face, I couldn't help but giggle.

"No way am I doing this next year," Owen said fervently. "But I can't just quit now that I'm on the team—that wouldn't be right."

"It wouldn't," I agreed. "You could tell Steve you don't want to spend all your free time doing something you hate, though."

Owen shrugged, and we stopped next to the car. Megan stuck her flag out the window and bonked him on the head.

"Batter up!" she yelled.

"All right, I'm coming." Swatting the flag away, Owen smiled at me. "Thanks for coming, by the way."

"Sure," I said. "It was fun."

"*Fun?*" he repeated, and I grinned.

"Well, it was less boring than a romance movie."

Owen laughed. "See you tomorrow, Holly."

"See you."

Chapter Six

On Friday, Mr. Dante showed us the schedule of our performance times for Solo and Ensemble Competition that weekend. My solo was at nine in the morning, but our trio wasn't scheduled till after eleven.

"Hallelujah," Liam said when he saw the list. "And my solo's in the afternoon. No waking up at the crack of dawn like all-region auditions." Then he gave me a sympathetic look. "Sorry your solo's so early."

"It's okay," I replied. Actually, I was relieved. The later the performance, the more time I'd have to get all nervous and freak myself out completely. Just like all-region auditions, Solo and Ensemble was for all the middle-school bands in the district. We weren't exactly in competition with one another, but I figured the judges would only give Superior ratings for the very best performances. Considering the cartwheels my stomach was turning when Mom dropped me off at Ridgewood on Saturday morning, it was a good thing I didn't have Liam's solo time. I'd never make it without puking.

I did a quick warm-up in the cafeteria and played through "Pastorale for Horn" once, then found the classroom that had been next to my name on the schedule. Mrs. Benitez held the door open for me.

"First solo of the day!" she said cheerfully. "Come on in."

"Thanks," I replied, stepping inside. When I saw who was sitting behind the judge's table, I stopped in my tracks. "Ms. Hunter!"

"Hi, Holly." The Bishop assistant band director glanced up from her papers and smiled. "How are you?"

"Good, thanks." I sat down in the chair next to the piano, still staring at her. "I didn't know you'd be . . . wait, do all the band directors in the region judge Solo and Ensemble?"

Ms. Hunter nodded. "Pretty much. Not for our own students, of course."

Huh. Since she was a horn player, it made sense that she'd be my judge. I wondered if Mr. Dante was judging in one of the low-brass rooms.

It helped a lot that I knew Ms. Hunter already. By the time Mrs. Benitez played the first few measures of "Pastorale," I was pretty relaxed. And not to brag or anything, but I kind of nailed my solo. When we finished, Ms. Hunter was grinning.

"Are you *sure* you have to go to Ridgewood?" she asked teasingly.

I blushed, laughing. "Yeah."

When I got back to the cafeteria, I spotted Owen and Max at one of the tables.

"How'd it go?" Owen asked, shuffling his Warlock cards.

"Great!" I told him about Ms. Hunter, since she'd be his judge, too. We played Warlock until it was time for Owen's solo. Not long after that, Natasha showed up, and she and Max went to warm up with Gabe and Victoria for their quartet. I got to see Julia for a few minutes before she played, and I talked Gabby out of devouring a package of M&M's before her solo. When I went to buy a soda, I ran into Nick's friend Rachel from Forest Hill at the vending machines. She told me he wasn't scheduled to play until later that afternoon, which was kind of a bummer. Although he hadn't called me after all, so maybe it would've been weird to run into him.

At ten forty-five, Liam joined me, plunking his tuba case down on the table.

"Hey, Holly," he said. "Have you seen Aaron yet?"

"Nope," I replied, fiddling with my bracelet and trying not to sound too nervous. We still had twenty-five minutes—plenty of time to warm up and make it to our room.

But that quickly went down to twenty minutes, then fifteen. Liam and I tried playing through "Triptych" once, but it sounded weird without the trumpet part. And ten minutes before our time slot, just as I was about to have a heart attack, Aaron hurried into the cafeteria.

"I'm really sorry," he said, and Liam shrugged.

"It's okay, you made it."

I smiled at Aaron, but I couldn't help feeling annoyed as we left the cafeteria. It would have been nice to at least play through the trio once together before the real performance.

Outside the classroom, Aaron set his case down and started rummaging through his backpack. His expression grew more and more troubled.

"I can't find my music," he said at last. "I swear I put it here yesterday . . ."

He emptied the contents of his bag onto the floor, and he and Liam started sorting through all the crumpled-up papers. I glanced up at the clock on the wall.

Six minutes. Stellar.

"Did you leave it in the practice room?" Liam asked.

"No . . . well, maybe." Aaron shook his head, flipping frantically through a binder. "I don't know, but it's not here."

Taking a deep breath, I glanced down the hall and spotted Ms. Hunter at a vending machine.

"Be right back," I told the guys before sprinting down the corridor.

I explained everything to Ms. Hunter, and she brought me to the band hall and found one of Ridgewood's band directors. He went straight to one of the filing cabinets in his office, and a few seconds later, he handed me the trumpet part to "Triptych."

"Just make sure you bring it back," he said with a smile.

"I will, I promise! Thank you!" Then I raced back to the classroom and thrust the part at Aaron just as the door opened and the room monitor stepped out.

"You guys ready?" he asked, giving me a strange look. Probably because I was doubled over, wheezing.

"Yeah."

Aaron stared at me. "Where did you get this?"

"Borrowed it," I said shortly, because I was still trying to catch my breath. And maybe I was a little irritated, too. I mean, how hard is it to just keep your music in a folder?

We walked into the classroom and took our seats. My heart was pounding way too fast, and Aaron and Liam both looked frazzled, too. So when we started "Triptych," the first few measures were a little shaky. But we settled into it, sort of. By the time we finished, I had no idea what to think. It wasn't a bad performance at all. It definitely wasn't our best, though.

"Nice job," the judge said with a smile. I wasn't sure I agreed.

"Man, I'm *really* sorry," Aaron said the second we were back in the hall. "I can't believe I lost my music."

"It's okay, it happens," Liam replied, setting his tuba down. "No big deal."

Aaron glanced down at the trumpet part, then

looked at me. "Who should I give this to?"

"Don't worry about it," I said, holding my hand out. "I got it from Ridgewood's band director—I'll bring it back."

"Okay, thanks." Aaron handed me the music. "And thanks for getting it, Holly. Sorry about all this."

"It's okay." I meant it, too, because he looked like he felt really bad.

Besides, we'd get another chance to perform "Triptych" on the band trip. That's what I told myself as I walked back to the band hall. Still . . . I couldn't help being bothered by the fact that after how much we'd practiced the trio, Aaron's lack of organizational skills might have cost us a good rating.

I worked on my research paper for English on Sunday afternoon until my brain started turning to mush. The first draft wasn't due for another week, but that was the band trip, so I had to have it done by Friday. Which wasn't exactly fair, in my opinion. I figured getting out of school to go to New Orleans would be totally worth it, though.

After three straight hours of reading about Eleanor Roosevelt's role in the civil rights movement, I closed my library books and threw myself facedown on my bed. When the phone rang, I grabbed it and held it to my ear without moving my head.

"'Erro?" My face was half-smushed in my pillow.

"Hi, is Holly there?" It was a boy.

"This is Holly."

"Oh, hi! This is Nick. From all-region."

I sat up straight, accidentally knocking the pillow off my bed. "Oh! Hey," I said, flustered. "What's up?"

"Not much," Nick replied. "I looked for you yesterday, but Rachel said your solo time was really early. How'd it go?"

"Pretty good," I said. "But the trio I was in ended up being kind of a train wreck."

"What happened?"

I told him the whole story. It felt kind of good to gripe about it, honestly. I didn't want to complain to Natasha about Aaron, and when I'd tried to call Julia last night, her dad said she was at the movies with Seth.

"It's just kind of frustrating, because we could've played it so much better," I finished. "Our rating probably won't be very good."

"I bet it will be," Nick replied. "Last year, I was in this quartet, and the week before Solo and Ensemble, Lisa—our tuba player—she got the flu. But she showed up that Saturday because she said she was feeling better, so we played it anyway, and . . ."

"It sounded bad?"

"Well, we were doing okay until about halfway through," said Nick. "Then we got to this part where Lisa had to hold out a really long note, and she kind of . . . sneezed. Into her mouthpiece."

I struggled not to laugh. "Ew."

"The worst part was the noise her tuba made," Nick went on, and I could tell he was grinning. "Even the judge laughed. We had to restart in the middle of the song."

"She must have felt horrible!" I said, even though I couldn't help giggling. "Not that she sneezed on purpose, but still."

"Yeah, she felt bad, but other than that we did okay," said Nick. "And the judge still gave us a really good rating. I bet yours will, too."

I smiled. "I hope so. So what about yesterday? How'd you do?"

"Pretty good. I—"

There was a *click*, and someone said: "Holly?"

Oh no.

"I'm using the phone, Chad." I tried not to sound too panicked. "Hang up!"

"I gotta call work to check my schedule," Chad said impatiently. "You hang up."

"Chad—"

"It's okay, Holly," said Nick. "I can call back later."

Before I could respond, Chad cut in. "Who's this?"

"It's my friend Nick," I said quickly. "For the love, Chad, can you just—"

"The guy you play video games with?"

"No, he's—"

"The guy you keep letting borrow all my DVDs?"

"No, just—"

"Geez, Holly!" Chad exclaimed. "How many boyfriends do you have?"

Oh my God.

My face burned. Before I could respond, I heard Dad yell, "Chad, leave her alone!"

"But I've gotta call work!" Chad yelled back.

"It's okay, I should go anyway." Nick sounded kind of freaked out. "Um, talk to you later, Holly."

"Bye," I managed to say right before he hung up. Immediately, Chad started dialing. *Beep-boop-boop–*

"Chad!" I cried. "What is *wrong* with you?"

"What?" He sounded confused. I could practically hear him squinting. "I told you, I gotta call work."

"You . . . you just . . . ," I sputtered. "Never mind."

Slamming the phone down, I sprawled back on my bed and covered my face with my hands. Well, that was completely mortifying. If I ever actually *did* get a boyfriend, no way was he ever meeting my brother.

Mr. Dante put up the results from Solo and Ensemble on Monday during band. I crossed my fingers behind my back, held my breath, and crowded around with everyone else. My eyes went to the sheet with solo results first.

Holly Mead—I (Superior)

My breath flew out in a whoosh, and I grinned. I knew I'd played well, but still—it was pretty cool to know that Ms. Hunter had thought so, too. I scanned the other solo results. It looked like almost everyone from Millican had gotten either a Superior or an Excellent rating. Gabby and Natasha both had Superior next to their names. No surprises there. But so did Owen! Beaming, I turned and peered around everyone until I spotted him over by the cubbies. I headed over to congratulate him when someone tugged on my arm.

"Guess I didn't mess us up too bad," Aaron said, smiling at me.

"What? Oh!" My eyes flew back to the results, and I quickly found my name on the ensemble list.

"Triptych"—*I (Superior)*

Aaron Cook

Holly Mead

Liam Park

"Wow!" I couldn't help sounding a little shocked. It looked like Nick had been right about the judge being forgiving. I would've called him to let him know if Chad hadn't scared him off.

Mr. Dante appeared next to me, digging through a bag of medals. He handed two to Aaron, then two to me. One for my solo, one for "Triptych." Stepping to the side, I stared at my medals, mentally rearranging my bulletin board to make room for them. I didn't notice Julia next to me until she poked my arm.

"Nice job!" she said with a grin.

"Thanks!" I smiled back. "Did you get your medals yet?"

"Just one. For my ensemble." Wrinkling her nose, Julia pointed at the results. "I didn't do as well on my solo."

I glanced at the solo list, my eyes widening a little.

Julia Gordon—II (Excellent)

"Oh!" Blinking, I turned back to Julia. "That's still good, though! I mean, technically it's *excellent*." As soon as I said it, I winced. What a lame thing to say. But Julia laughed.

"It's okay, I'm not upset." She shrugged. "Honestly,

I didn't practice it as much as I probably should have. I just didn't have the time."

I thought about the study lockdown Julia's parents had imposed a few weeks ago because of her grade in history, and how Natasha and I barely saw her anymore. It seemed like Seth was the *only* thing Julia had time for now—never mind school, band, or her friends.

But I didn't say any of that, of course. I just patted her sympathetically on the arm and tucked my medals safely in my pocket.

𝄞

The week before the band trip was nothing but essays, tests, piles of homework, and absolutely no alien carnage. Poor Owen had it even worse than I did, with baseball practices and another game on top of everything else. On the bright side, that weekend was Julia's surprise party.

On Saturday morning, Mom and I got up early to do a little shopping. We stumbled into the kitchen at noon, weighed down with bags of decorations, groceries, and Julia's birthday present—a giant jewelry-making kit that came with lots of colored glass beads and pendants.

By two o'clock, everyone was at my house. Natasha and I had invited Gabby, Victoria Rios, and Leah Collins. We got to work hanging streamers, blowing up balloons, and making an enormous coconut cake. Julia's dad, who pretty much could've been a professional chef, lent me a bunch of tools to make frosting flowers. We kind of went overboard.

"This thing is more frosting than cake," Gabby said cheerfully, piping out a purple tulip. I nodded in agreement. It looked like a giant basket of slightly misshapen but colorful flowers in the middle of the counter.

"We should probably stop," Natasha murmured as she added tiny green leaves along the bottom edge of the cake.

"Yeah." Holding the finished tulip in her palm, Gabby eyed the cake. Then she popped the tulip into her mouth. "Mmmm, frosting." She grinned at us, revealing purple-stained teeth, and we laughed.

"It's almost five," I said, glancing at the clock. "We should probably order the pizza soon—Julia's supposed to get here in an hour."

As I was digging through a drawer of takeout menus, looking for the one from Spins, the back door flew open. Chad took a few steps and stopped, his eyes wide.

"What the . . ."

I snickered as he looked from the girls crowded around the counter to the ridiculous frosting-flower monstrosity. "Julia's surprise party," I said. "I *told* you about this yesterday."

"Did not."

Rolling my eyes, I pulled out the Spins menu, then swatted Chad's hand when he tried to swipe a bit of frosting off the cake. "Gross!" I yelled. "Seriously, Chad—get out of here. Go over to Leon's or something."

"All right, all right," he grumbled, heading to the living room. The phone rang just as he got to the door, and he grabbed it before I could. "Hello? . . . Yeah, hang on." Chad held the phone out. "For you. And it's actually *not* a boy this time."

I took the phone, then shoved Chad out of the kitchen.

"What boy is he talking about?" Gabby asked immediately.

"Ugh, I'll tell you later," I said before putting the phone to my ear. "Hello?"

"Hey, it's me!"

Frantically, I waved at the others, then put my hand over the mouthpiece. "It's Julia!" I hissed, and they fell quiet.

"Hi!" I said. "Are you on your way over?"

"Holly, you won't believe this!" Julia exclaimed. "Guess what Seth surprised me with for my birthday?"

"What?"

"Tickets to see *Infinite Crush*!"

"Wow!" *Way to go, Seth,* I thought with a grin. Infinite Crush was one of Julia's favorite bands.

"I know, I can't believe it!" Julia went on breathlessly. "I've got to figure out what to wear, too. I'm really sorry about dinner, but do you want to come over and help me pick something out?"

I blinked a few times. "What?"

"I was thinking that green dress I got for Christmas, but I'm not sure which shoes—"

"No, wait." Ducking through the doorway into the living room, I lowered my voice. "Julia, the concert's *tonight?*"

"Yeah!"

"But . . ." I stared around the living room at all the streamers and balloons. A huge banner stretched on the wall over the couch—Natasha and Gabby had spent almost an hour writing HAPPY BIRTHDAY, JULIA with little music note stamps. "You're supposed to come over."

"I know, and I'm *really* sorry, but can't we do dinner tomorrow?" Julia asked. "Holly, it's *Infinite Crush!* The tickets are for tonight—I can't just see them another time."

"Yeah, but the thing is . . ." Hesitating, I glanced back in the kitchen. Everyone was still joking and laughing, piling more frosting flowers on the cake. "Well, I was kind of going to surprise you, too."

"What?"

"It's a surprise slumber party," I told her. "Natasha's here, and Gabby, and we made a cake . . ."

"Oh!" Julia was quiet for a second. "Wow, Holly, I didn't—I mean, thank you! That's so cool!"

I grinned, relieved. "You're welcome! Just pretend to be surprised when you get here, okay?" When she didn't respond, my smile faded. "Julia?"

"But, Holly . . ." Julia sounded nervous. "I can't

come. I mean . . . the concert."

"What?"

"I'm *so* sorry, but it's not like I knew!" she said quickly. "I had no idea Seth got these tickets, and I didn't know about the party, either."

"Right, we both surprised you." I stared at the banner, gripping the phone a little too hard. "And you're picking Seth."

"Holly, come on! The concert's only tonight—we can do a slumber party anytime."

My mouth fell open. Because she actually sounded irritated.

"You're right," I snapped. "After all, we're just your best friends. Your boyfriend is obviously way more important, so just—just go to the concert. Have fun."

I hung up before she could respond. My hands were shaking.

Tears pricked the corners of my eyes, and I squeezed them shut. I could hear the girls giggling about something in the kitchen. What was I supposed to tell them? *Sorry, guys, but Julia's got better things to do.*

Suddenly, I felt more angry than hurt. Wiping my eyes, I headed back into the kitchen and set the phone on the counter.

"Check it out!" Gabby pulled me over to the cake, pointing. The words *Happy Birthday* were scrawled in almost illegible script, taking up pretty much the entire mound of flowers. Crammed in beneath, a tiny yellow squiggle covered a cluster of frosting leaves.

"That says *Julia*, I just ran out of room," Gabby said defensively when I squinted. Natasha and the others snickered. "Hey, it still looks good!" Gabby cried. "Julia will love it."

"Actually," I told her, swiping a bit of frosting and licking my finger, "Julia's not coming. So we might as well just put more flowers on it."

"What?"

Picking up a bag of red frosting, I started piping out an enormous rose. "Yeah, apparently Seth surprised her with tickets to see Infinite Crush tonight, so . . ." With a shrug, I plopped the rose on top of the yellow squiggle. "She's not coming."

I glanced up at Natasha, whose mouth was open. "Are you serious?"

"Yeah."

Cue the awkward silence. My eyes fell on the Spins menu, and I picked it up.

"Anyway, what should I order?" Ugh, my voice sounded all perky and weird. But Gabby took the menu and flipped it open.

"Cinnamon sticks," she announced. "Oh, and they've got that chocolate-cherry dessert pizza . . ."

"Dude, we already have a mountain of frosting!" Victoria pointed to our coconut cake monstrosity, and I relaxed a little bit. While she and Leah tried to talk Gabby into eating pepperoni like a normal human being, Natasha came around the counter.

"So she's really not coming?" she asked softly.

"Yeah." I kept my voice low. "And she was actually *annoyed* when I told her about the party."

Natasha's eyes widened. "*What?*"

"I mean, not about the party," I corrected myself. "But I figured once I told her about it, she'd come, you know? And she just said *we can do a slumber party anytime.*"

Wrinkling her nose, Natasha poked a frosting bag. "Well, glad we went to all this trouble."

"I know."

"Hey, Holly—are these yours?"

I glanced up to see Victoria waving something at me. My Warlock cards.

"Oh, yeah," I replied. "Owen gave me those. It's this game we play at lunch."

"Yeah, I've got some, too!" she said.

"Really?"

"I've got study hall with Max and Trevor, so we play sometimes." Victoria headed for the door. "Actually, I think mine are in my backpack."

After ordering the pizza (and cinnamon sticks for Gabby), I joined the others in the living room. They were sprawled in a circle on the floor, examining the Warlock cards. Victoria was trying to explain the rules, but Gabby kept yelling things like "look, a rhino-dude!" and waving her tusked-warrior card in Leah's face. Laughing, I sat down next to Natasha and grabbed my set of cards. When Victoria started going over the types of spells and potions with the others, I leaned over to Natasha.

"We have to talk to Julia," I said quietly. "This whole picking Seth over us thing . . . I don't know, maybe she doesn't realize she's doing it."

"Well . . ." Natasha frowned. "It's not her fault Seth surprised her the same night as us. She probably just doesn't get how much work we put into this, you know? I mean, if she saw everyone here right now, with all the decorations and the cake and stuff . . ."

I thought about it. "Yeah, she'd probably feel really bad. And I mean, it *would* be sad if she had to miss that concert." Then I sighed. I didn't want to fight with Julia, even if she really had hurt my feelings. "The trip's this week, too."

Natasha crinkled her nose. "Right. Ugh, I don't want things to be weird with Julia—New Orleans is going to be so much fun!"

I nodded. "So let's talk to her Monday and explain everything, okay? I'm sure she'll understand."

"Definitely." Natasha squinted at one of her cards. "And Holly?"

"Yeah?"

She waved the card at me—an angry-looking and very dirty gnome climbing out of an unlit fireplace. "This game is really weird."

"That's a chimney gnome. They have magic brooms."

Natasha's eyebrow arched, and I laughed. "Just give it a chance! I'll show you how to play."

Teaching everyone Warlock turned out to be a good

distraction. The rest of the night was fun—I mean, we had pizza, a cake piled with frosting, and lots of movies (although all of my suggestions were unanimously vetoed). But every once in a while, Natasha and I would glance at each other, and I knew she was thinking about Julia, too. Wondering if she was having fun at the concert with Seth. If she cared at all that she'd hurt our feelings.

But I felt a little better the next morning. Natasha had to be right—Julia was just caught off guard with the party and the concert tickets. We could fix this. We just had to talk to her.

After a breakfast of doughnuts and orange juice, everyone's parents came to pick them up. I cleaned up the living room, then spent the rest of the day having a horror movie marathon with Chad. It was kind of meditative, really. Maybe my best friend was being a little selfish, but hey—there were no ghosts living in my bathroom mirror, and Chad's car wasn't possessed by a demon.

Things could be worse.

Chapter Eight

When I saw Natasha before band on Monday, I started to think maybe I was wrong.

"Julia barely said two words to me in history this morning," Natasha whispered while I took my horn out of its case. "It's like she's actually *mad* at us."

I glanced around the cubbies. No Julia yet.

"Well, she probably thinks *we're* mad at *her*," I said. "I mean, I did sort of yell at her on the phone. I *was* mad. We just need to talk to her."

"We have to do it right after band, then," Natasha replied as we headed to our seats. "Seth will be at lunch."

I made a face. "Yeah, that would be awkward. Okay, after band."

When we sat down, Owen came out of Mr. Dante's office holding something behind his back. He looked like he was trying not to smile.

"What's that?" I asked as soon as he reached his chair.

"Nothing." Owen glanced around, then slid over into Brooke's empty chair next to Natasha. "Okay, our band shirts came in."

"Oh!" Leaning closer, I watched eagerly as he unrolled the shirt.

Last semester, we'd held a band bake sale to raise money for our trip to New Orleans. Mr. Dante promised that the section who earned the most money would get to pick the design for our new band shirts. Since the brass section won, we'd decided to have Owen come up with something original.

It had been my idea. And apparently, it was a good one.

"Awesome!" I exclaimed, right as Natasha said, "Wow!"

The middle of the shirt was an explosion of instruments, flutes and horns and drumsticks all bursting out in a circle—it almost looked 3-D. A confetti of music notes and clefs surrounded the instruments, with MILLICAN MIDDLE SCHOOL in a curve along the top of the circle and BAND in huge letters along the bottom.

"Whoa, did you *draw* that?"

We turned to see Aaron leaning out of his chair, his eyes wide. Victoria stood up to see, then Trevor, and pretty soon half the band was crowded around us. Owen's face was red.

"Yeah," he said. "Well, it started as a sketch, but then I scanned it and used a program to do the color wash and adjust the tonal gradation and . . ." He trailed off, looking embarrassed. "I mean, yeah, I drew it."

"That is *so cool!*" Gabby exclaimed right as Mr. Dante dropped a box on his podium. "Is that our shirts?" she asked eagerly, and he smiled.

"Yes—and if you'll take your seats, maybe I can hand them out."

I reached across Natasha to nudge Owen's arm before he slid back over to his seat. "Nice job!"

He grinned, still a little red-faced. "Thanks."

Mr. Dante went over our schedule and packing list for the band trip while Sophie and Liam passed out the shirts. In all the excitement, I'd almost forgotten about Julia. She was staring at her schedule, T-shirt in her lap. I watched her for a minute, but she never looked up.

"Okay, warm-ups," Mr. Dante announced. "And after we take care of the chair test, let's do a run-through of all three pieces for the contest."

I froze with my hand on my folder. *Chair test?* Glancing around, I realized no one else looked surprised. Then I remembered.

Our next chair test will be the day before the trip. Mr. Dante had told us last week. Numbly, I pulled out my scale sheet. I'd *never* forgotten about a chair test before.

After warm-ups, Mr. Dante tested the woodwinds one at a time while I practically burned a hole through the exercise with my eyes. It wasn't too hard, but I hadn't played through it in almost a week. Ugh, this was so unlike me.

When it was Natasha's turn, I held my horn in my

lap, quietly pressing the valves down along with her. I messed up a rhythm in the fourth measure, then noticed the key signature and realized I'd been playing B naturals instead of B flats the whole time. So when my turn came, I was pretty much freaking out in my head.

And I totally bombed.

Okay, it wasn't catastrophic or anything. It wasn't like the time at the pep rally when I had to play a solo in front of the whole school and the grossest noise *ever* came out of my horn. But it was by far the worst I'd ever done on a chair test.

Right before the band trip, too. Stellar.

When Mr. Dante had moved on to Brooke, I leaned closer to Natasha. "Oh my God."

She smiled. "Aw, it wasn't *that* bad." I gave her a Look, and she snickered.

Brooke sounded pretty good. I listened carefully as Owen played. He'd seemed pretty surprised about getting a Superior rating on his solo, especially since he spent so much time at baseball practice now. But obviously he was still finding time to practice for band, because he sounded great on the chair test, too.

Owen could probably teach Julia something about time management. It was kind of a mean thing to think, but I thought it anyway.

After rehearsal, I noticed Julia lingering at her cubby, slowly taking her clarinet apart and placing the pieces in her case. I took my time, too, waiting while

Natasha talked to Aaron. Once he'd left the cubby room, Natasha and I headed over to Julia.

"Hey!" I said, keeping my voice light. Julia glanced at us.

"Hi."

"Look, we just wanted to talk to you about Saturday," I told her, and Natasha nodded. "I'm sorry about what I said, but I was upset—Natasha and I planned that party for weeks, we had all these people over decorating all day, and we made this cake, and it just—"

"Oh my God, stop!" Julia's eyes squinched up, and I couldn't tell if she was about to cry or was just glaring at me. "Geez, Holly, what's with the guilt trip about this party? It's not my fault—I didn't *know*!"

I stared at her. "Guilt trip?"

"Yes!" She let out a shaky breath. "You planned a surprise party for me and I didn't come, and I'm really sorry, seriously . . . but on the phone, you made me feel horrible! You said I picked Seth, like I chose him over you guys."

"You *did*!"

"That's not fair!" she cried. I glanced around, but the cubby room was empty. "Just because I went to the concert instead? It's not like—"

"Hang on," Natasha interrupted. "Julia, I'm really sorry, but it's . . . it's not *just* because you went to the concert."

Julia wiped her eyes. "What do you mean?"

Natasha and I shared a glance. "You just . . ." I

chewed my lip. "You spend a lot of time with Seth now, which is great, but it just seems like we never see you anymore."

"And when we do, he's all you want to talk about," Natasha added. "Or you'll make plans with us, then not show up because of Seth—like when we were supposed to have lunch at my place before all-region."

"We're really happy you like him so much," I said quickly. "We just . . . I don't know, we miss you. And sometimes, like Saturday, it feels like you'd rather hang out with Seth than us."

Julia's eyes welled up with tears, and suddenly I felt terrible. She really must not have known how she'd been treating us lately. It would feel pretty awful to suddenly realize you'd been neglecting your best friends.

"Why are you guys being so mean?" she whispered.

My mouth dropped. "What?"

"You're being *mean*." Julia wiped her eyes, her voice hardening. "Yeah, I hang out with Seth a lot. Do you yell at Natasha when she goes out with Aaron?"

"Of course not!" I felt my cheeks heat up, and Natasha cut in.

"Julia, this is different," she said. "It's not just that you hang out with him a lot, it's . . ."

"It's that you *always* choose him over us," I finished. "Every single time."

"Based on Saturday?" Julia snapped. "You know, those tickets were expensive, and it's not like I planned for the concert to be that night. It's not my fault—I didn't know about it. Or the slumber party."

"Fine, I get that." I took a deep, shaky breath. "But it's not like that mattered. We could've told you about the party weeks ago, and I bet you still would've ditched us for Seth."

Julia shook her head and picked up her backpack. "You know what? I don't have to listen to this." And she stormed out of the cubby room.

Natasha and I looked at each other in disbelief.

"I can't believe she's mad at us," I said, my voice quaking a little. "We haven't done anything wrong!"

Natasha shook her head. "I know."

We didn't say much as we walked to the cafeteria. Julia sat with Seth, facing away from the entrance. Natasha and I were heading to our regular table when I noticed Aaron waving. Natasha saw him, too, and waved back before turning to me.

"Um, do you want to come sit with me and Aaron?" she asked. "His friends won't mind, and—"

"Nah, go ahead!" I said before she could finish. "No, really, you go. It's Warlock time, anyway."

Natasha gave me a halfhearted smile. "You and that weird game."

She made her way over to Aaron's table, and I plopped down next to Owen and threw my lunch bag on the table probably a little harder than necessary.

"Watch it!" Trevor gave me a dirty look, stacking up the pile of cards I'd knocked over.

"Sorry," I muttered. Owen grabbed the stack and started shuffling them.

"Something wrong?" he asked.

"Nope." Sighing, I pulled out my sandwich, along with my deck of cards. "Let's play."

𝄞

Julia and I didn't speak for the rest of the day. Not even in computer lab seventh period—she sat on the other side of the room. I just couldn't believe she was so angry, like Natasha and I had done something wrong.

I fumed all the way home and all through dinner. But then I started packing for New Orleans, which turned out to be a pretty good distraction.

"What in the . . ."

Chad stood in the doorway to my room, gawking. I'd pinned the packing list Mr. Dante had given us to my bulletin board, along with a list of my own. My bed was covered in neat stacks of folded clothes. My horn, cleaning supplies, and music were arranged on the floor. Shampoo, toothpaste, and all my other bathroom stuff were separated into labeled plastic baggies on my dresser. I kneeled on the floor in front of a row of every pair of shoes I owned, in order by type.

"I'm busy, Chad."

Chad squinted. "Are you seriously bringing all those shoes?"

"Of course not." I rolled my eyes. "I'm narrowing it down to three pairs."

"Holly," Chad said slowly. "You make packing *way* too complicated. I'd have this done in five minutes."

I snorted. "Right, like when we went to the lake for a week last summer."

"Exactly."

"Chad, you forgot to pack underwear."

He shrugged. "So? I had swim trunks, it didn't matter."

Shaking my head, I set aside two pairs of sandals and moved on to sneakers. "Never mind. What do you want?"

"Do you know where my *Scattered* DVD is?"

I pointed to my dresser. "There. Hang on," I added when he stepped forward. "Are you lending it to someone?"

Grabbing the case, Chad sighed. "Yeah, Toby. And no, I'm not making him sign that stupid sheet you made."

"Fine, but you'd better mark down that he borrowed it in that spreadsheet I sent you."

"Yeah, I'll do that."

I glared at Chad as he headed back into the hall. "Are you being sarcastic?"

"Oh no. Of course not." He closed my door behind him with a little smirk.

Seriously, between his total lack of organizational skills and his fear of washing machines, it would be a miracle if my brother survived college.

Chapter Nine

I woke up ten minutes before my six o'clock alarm went off. Thirty minutes later, I'd hauled my luggage, backpack, and horn case down to the kitchen. Mom walked in and flipped on the coffeemaker. Then she saw me by the door and groaned.

"Holly . . ."

"I know," I interrupted. "The charter bus doesn't leave until eight. But look." I waved Mr. Dante's schedule at her, then read out loud: "*Be there early—if you sleep in, you'll be left behind.*"

Mom opened her mouth, then closed it and shook her head. I watched as she traded her coffee mug for a thermos. Five minutes later, we were in the car, pulling out of the driveway.

The school's parking lot was deserted. I squinted at the clock—it wasn't even seven yet. Leaning back in her seat, Mom took a sip of coffee and gave me the side-eye.

"Better safe than sorry," I told her firmly, and she grumbled something under her breath.

Half an hour later, a few more cars pulled into the parking lot. I saw Mr. Dante walking up to unlock the band hall just as a huge charter bus appeared at the end of the street.

Once the bus parked, Mom helped me drag all my stuff over. "Got your cell phone?"

"Yup." I set my horn case down, pulled my phone out of my pocket, and waved it at her.

"Have a great time, be safe, don't forget to . . ." She paused, yawning. "Call me when you get there. Oh, there's Julia!"

I turned instinctively as Mom waved. Mr. Gordon waved back from his car, where Julia was pulling her suitcase out of the backseat. I faced Mom again.

"Thanks, Mom. Love you." We hugged, and the second she headed back to her car, I hurried to the band hall. Seeing Julia had my stomach all knotted up. We'd been looking forward to the band trip for months, and now we weren't even speaking to each other.

Mr. Dante stood just inside the band hall, taping a few sheets to the door.

"Good morning, Holly."

"Morning," I said. "What's that?"

"Room assignments," he explained. "I'll go over them again when we get to the hotel, but I thought everyone would want to see them before we leave."

Oh no. I tried to smile at Mr. Dante as he headed

to his office. A few weeks ago, everyone had put in roommate requests. I found my name on the list and groaned.

Room 5

Gabby Flores

Natasha Prynne

Holly Mead

Julia Gordon

Stellar. I couldn't *believe* I'd forgotten we'd be rooming together. Especially since I'd been so excited about it—five whole days with Julia, and no Seth. Frustrated, I leaned my head against the door that led out to the parking lot. Then someone pulled it open, and I stumbled forward with a shriek.

"Holly!" Natasha caught me, laughing. "You okay?"

"Yeah." I made a face. "Well, not really. Look."

I pointed to the list and watched Natasha wince. "Oh, right. Forgot about that." She glanced around, lowering her voice. "This is stupid. I don't want to fight with Julia. Maybe we can talk to her on the bus ride or something."

"I don't really know if she wants to talk to us," I said. "But you're right—we should try. Again."

By now, it looked like most of the band was here. After Natasha grabbed her horn from the cubbies, we headed back outside. A few parents were loading all the luggage and instrument cases into the compartment under the bus. Liam's mom stood near the door, holding a clipboard.

"Morning, ladies!" she said cheerfully.

"Hi, Mrs. Park."

"Natasha and Holly." She added two checks to her list and smiled at us. "Lucky me, you're in one of the rooms I'm chaperoning. I know I won't have any problems with you girls!"

We smiled back and headed up the steps.

"Is Julia on yet?" I asked, standing on tiptoe. The charter bus was *huge*, and several kids were still milling around, looking for seats.

"I don't see . . . oh. Yeah." Natasha glanced at me. "Look, she's way back there, next to Sophie. The seats around her are already taken."

I sighed. "Great."

Natasha and I headed down the aisle. I was about to grab two empty seats together when Natasha turned around to face me, her expression worried.

"Um, Holly . . . ," she said hesitantly. "I kind of promised Aaron I'd sit with him."

"Oh!" I almost laughed. Of course she'd want to sit with her boyfriend. "No problem."

"I don't have to, though!" she added quickly. "Why don't we just—"

"No, don't be ridiculous." When I spotted Aaron, I pushed Natasha gently down the aisle. "Sit with him, seriously."

"Are you sure?"

"Yes! I'll find you guys when we stop for lunch, okay?"

"Okay." Natasha gave me a grateful smile. I stepped to the side to let Max pass, then faced the front of the bus. Noticing the top of a blond head in the second row, I made my way up the aisle.

"Hey!" I said. "Can I sit with you?"

"Sure!" Owen heaved his stuffed backpack off the seat next to him. I sat down, staring at the bag.

"Geez, what did you bring?"

Instead of answering, he unzipped the backpack and held it open. I peered inside and grinned. Sketchbook, a giant pack of pencils, some sort of a handheld video game, a stack of DVDs, and a bunch of snacks. It was like Owen had somehow packed his whole game room into his bag.

"Why the movies?" I asked.

"To watch on the ride." Owen pointed, and sure enough, there was a DVD player installed between the front window and the ceiling. Then I noticed little flip-down TVs over the seats, like on an airplane.

"Aw, I should've brought some of mine!"

Owen smiled. "I don't think Mr. Dante would let us watch any of your movies."

Before I could respond, someone said: "Why not?" We both glanced up to see Mr. Dante putting his laptop bag in the seat behind the driver.

"She only owns horror movies," Owen explained, and Mr. Dante raised an eyebrow at me.

"Horror movies are perfect for a trip," I said defensively. "Do you have any idea how many of them start out like this, with a group of people going on vacation or something, and then their car breaks down in a little town that's haunted or has a bunch of vampires or—"

"Holly," Mr. Dante interrupted. "I'm pretty sure most of the students—and parents—would very much *not* enjoy watching a movie like that during a long bus ride."

I sighed. "Yeah. Not many people have good taste in movies."

Snickering, Owen pulled one of the DVDs out of his bag and handed it to Mr. Dante. "How about this one?"

"*Cyborgs versus Ninjas*." Mr. Dante flipped the case over and read the back. "This looks fine. I don't think Holly agrees, though," he added, probably because I was scowling.

"No, it's a good movie," I admitted grudgingly. "Even if the title is totally misleading."

"She tried to guess the ending," Owen told Mr. Dante. "And failed."

I glared at him. Laughing, Mr. Dante slid the case on top of the DVD player. "Okay, this one will be up first. Let's get everyone settled in and go over a few rules first, though."

While Mrs. Park did one last head count, Owen took out his sketchbook and a pencil. He whistled a little as he flipped it open to a sketch of a bunch of different superheroes.

"You're in a good mood," I said, watching him draw.

Owen nodded without looking up. "Five days with no baseball!"

I smiled. "Yeah." After a few seconds, I cleared my throat. "So are you going to enter that art contest?"

His pencil kept moving, but I saw him blink a few times. "Actually, um . . . I kind of already did. A few weeks ago, right after we talked about it in science class. I figured I'd better do it before the first baseball—" He jumped when I clapped once, loudly.

"You *entered*!" I cried. "That's awesome! When will you find out the results?"

"They said four to six weeks."

"Let's see, I remember us talking about it the week before all-region . . ." Quickly, I counted the weeks on my fingers. "So there's a chance you could hear something this week, then?"

"Yeah, maybe." Owen tapped his pencil on the pad. "There were a ton of entries, though. Like, hundreds. So chances are—"

"Chances are, you'll destroy them all," I said firmly. He laughed, blushing.

"Thanks."

Mrs. Park passed us and stopped in front of Mr. Dante's seat. "Only one student hasn't shown up yet," she said. "Trevor Wells."

I saw Mr. Dante glance at his watch. "Well, he's got three minutes."

"Oh my God, are we actually going to leave him if he doesn't show up in three minutes?" I blurted out, and they both looked up, startled. Mr. Dante pushed his glasses up his nose, giving me a serious look.

"Absolutely," he said. "In fact, we might leave in two minutes. My instructions were to get here early, after all."

I gaped at him for a few seconds before realizing Mrs. Park was laughing. "You're just messing with me, aren't you.""

Mr. Dante shook his head solemnly, but Mrs. Park winked at me.

"Some kids just can't do mornings," she said, sighing. "I practically have to turn the garden hose on Liam to get him out of bed."

"That's how Trevor is," Owen told her. "His mom puts an alarm clock outside his door so he actually has to get up and walk across the room to turn it off."

Mrs. Park arched an eyebrow. "I'm surprised he even hears it. Liam could sleep through an earthquake."

"It's not a normal alarm," Owen said with a grin. "He showed me once—it sounds like a police siren or an air horn or something."

"Interesting," Mrs. Park mused. "I should look into that."

Someone rapped on the bus doors, and the driver leaned over to open them. Trevor stumbled up the stairs, dragging his backpack. His clothes were wrinkled, his hair stuck out all over the place, and his eyes looked all squinty and watery.

"I'm here," he mumbled. Owen and I laughed, and

Mrs. Park shook her head.

"Barely made it," she said, checking him off the list. "Okay, we're ready to go!"

Trevor collapsed into the seats behind me and Owen. The snoring started before the bus even pulled out of the parking lot.

Chapter Ten

For the first half hour, the bus ride was *loud*. Everyone (well, except Trevor, obviously) was talking and joking around, and the good mood was contagious—I even started to feel better about Julia. Natasha and I would just have to talk to her when we checked into our room. By the time we went to dinner tonight, we'd be friends again.

While Owen sketched, I tried playing the handheld game he'd brought. It wasn't nearly as much fun as *Prophets*, though. The chatter started to die down once we got on the highway, and before long, Trevor wasn't the only one snoring. My eyelids started to droop, too, and when my character died on the same level for the fifth time, I set the game in my lap to rest my eyes.

An hour later, I woke up with my head on Owen's shoulder.

Wait. *What*?

I stayed perfectly still, opening my eyes just a little

bit. He was still sketching, his right hand flying over the paper. His left arm was sort of pinned in. By me. Apparently, I'd slumped over on him from my seat while I slept. Well, this was awkward.

Awkward, but also kind of nice.

Not that I'd ever tell anyone that—Julia and Natasha would totally take it the wrong way. Besides, Owen was probably really uncomfortable. And if anyone saw the two of us right now, we'd never hear the end of it. I said a silent prayer of thanks that Trevor was still snoring away behind us. But any second, someone could come to the front to talk to Mr. Dante.

Like Gabby.

I squinted at the giant mirror over the driver's head, watching Gabby make her way down the aisle. She stopped next to Natasha and Aaron for a few seconds, and I noticed something in her hand—a DVD.

Okay, time to move. I just had to figure out the least awkward way to do it. The last thing I needed was for things to get all weird with Owen, like the whole winter dance catastrophe last semester.

But that was my fault for acting like a total spaz. This time, I'd do the opposite—play it cool. This was no big deal, sleeping on Owen's shoulder. I hadn't been lying here for the last five minutes freaking out about it. I'd just woken up, and everything was totally fine.

Yawning, I stretched and sat up. "Sorry," I said in the most casual voice possible, as if I'd only realized right this second that we'd practically been cuddling.

"Oh, is that for our science project?"

Owen nodded, tilting the sketchbook so I could get a better look at the roller coaster whipping a carful of aliens around a loop-the-loop. It was like the one I'd found online and printed for our proposal, only a million times cooler. His sketches were getting better, I realized. From awesome to mega-awesome.

"It's not very scientific, though." His voice sounded normal. So far, so good. "But it could just be part of the visual aids or something."

"Nice!" I chanced a peek at his face as he went back to drawing. Were his cheeks a little pink? No, it was probably my imagination. I breathed a little sigh of relief. Crisis averted.

Then it dawned on me that maybe Owen really *hadn't* minded the almost-cuddling. Maybe he even thought it was kind of nice, like I did. I glanced at him again, but he was focused on his sketchbook. *Overthinking things,* I told myself, leaning back in my chair. Owen was just being polite, letting me sleep on his shoulder. What else was he going to do, shove me in the aisle?

"Hey, guys!" Gabby appeared next to us, hopping up and down. I grinned up at her.

"How much sugar have you had?"

"Two bags of M&M's and a package of Twizzlers," Gabby said. "I've got a giant Ziploc full of carrot and celery sticks, if anyone wants it," she added, and I laughed. Across the aisle, Mrs. Park glanced up from her book to give Gabby a look of mixed disapproval and amusement.

"What movie did you bring?" Owen asked, and Gabby held it up.

"*Push Your Luck*," I read. "Never heard of it."

"It's *hilarious*," Gabby said fervently, then spun around and held the case out to Mr. Dante. He glanced up from his laptop, pushing his glasses up his nose.

"Looks okay," he said. "Although that robot movie—"

"Cyborgs," Owen and I corrected him at the same time.

"*Cyborg* movie," Mr. Dante went on, "is up first. But I don't want to start it while everyone's sleeping."

"Gotcha." Turning to face the back of the bus, Gabby sucked in a huge breath and hollered: "*Y'all wake up so we can watch a movie!*"

Owen and I laughed as a grungy tennis shoe flew over our heads, smacking Gabby in the arm. Behind us, Trevor mumbled something incoherent, shifting into a more comfortable position. His feet stuck out in the aisle—one shoe, one sock with a giant hole in the big toe. Gabby pulled off the sock and used it to swat him on the legs, which turned into a sock tug-of-war.

Mr. Dante massaged his temples. "It's going to be a long week," he told Mrs. Park, who nodded wearily.

He sent Gabby back to her seat and put *Cyborgs* in the DVD player. As soon as the opening credits started, Owen put his sketchbook away and pulled out a box of crackers. Trevor went back to snoring, even through the loudest explosions.

"I mean, seriously," I said about halfway through the movie. "The aliens built the cyborgs, so they're the actual bad guys. It should be called *Aliens versus Ninjas*."

"That would kind of spoil the twist, though." Owen sounded amused. "And apparently it's a pretty good twist, considering even you couldn't figure it out."

I flicked a cracker at him. He deflected it with the box, grinning.

After stopping for lunch at a taco place, Mr. Dante put in Gabby's movie. It *was* pretty funny (although totally predictable). But I was too distracted to pay much attention. Natasha and I had tried to find Julia in the restaurant, but we didn't see her until everyone started boarding the bus again. She was obviously determined to avoid us.

Not that she'd be able to for long. We'd just have to talk to her in our hotel room before dinner.

Victoria and Max came up to the front of the bus with their Warlock cards to join me, Owen, and Trevor. After about an hour, Leah and Gabe moved up a few seats. Pretty soon, we had a game going with almost a dozen players, all swapping cards over the chairs and across the aisle. I reached over Trevor's head to take Leah's charmed-goblet card.

"Hey, Holly?" Leah kept her voice low, even though Trevor was too busy arguing with Victoria to hear.

"Yeah?"

"Is everything okay with Julia?" she asked.

I tried to keep my face neutral. "Yeah, why?"

Leah shrugged. "Well, you looked kind of upset Saturday when she didn't show up to the party. And . . ."

"And?" I prompted.

"Well . . . Sophie told me that Julia told her you and Natasha yelled at her for hanging out with her boyfriend too much."

My mouth fell open. "*What?*" I hissed. "That's not true—we didn't *yell* at her!"

"Holly, it's your turn." Trevor was staring up at me impatiently. I looked down at my cards.

"Here." I tossed one at him, then turned back to Leah.

"A red saber?" Trevor sputtered. "Are you serious? You should hang on to this."

I waved him off. "Yeah, whatever, take it. Leah, that is *so* not what happened! We were just—"

"I need everyone back to their seats and facing the front, please."

Mr. Dante stood next to the driver, his brow furrowed. And suddenly I realized that the bus had slowed down, even though we were still on the highway. Leah gave me an apologetic look before heading back to her seat. I put my cards away, my fingers still trembling a little. What was going on with Julia, seriously? It's not like this was our first fight, but she'd *never* gossiped to someone else about me like that. Especially not Sophie.

"We're pulling over," Owen said, peering out the

window. "But I saw a sign a few minutes ago—New Orleans is still over a hundred miles away."

"There's nothing here but cornfields." I leaned past Owen to look up and down the street. We stopped on the edge of the road, close to the long fence that ran along the fields. The driver hopped off the bus and pulled out a cell phone, while Mrs. Park joined Mr. Dante at the front. Straining to hear them over all the other chatter, I caught the words *engine* and *mechanic*.

"Is the bus broken?" I blurted out. "Are we stranded in the middle of nowhere?"

Mr. Dante smiled reassuringly. "There's a small problem with the bus, but don't worry, Holly—we aren't stranded."

"I'm not worried!" I exclaimed, my anger and hurt over Julia temporarily forgotten. "This is *awesome*! It's just like in *House of the Wicked*, how there's this graveyard close to the house and anytime a car drives by at night it gets a flat tire and—"

I stopped talking when the driver stepped back on the bus, and Mr. Dante and Mrs. Park looked relieved. The three of them spoke quietly for a few seconds, then Mr. Dante turned around and cleared his throat.

"Okay, guys," he said, and the chatter died down. "We're having a minor problem with the engine. The mechanic's on his way, so just sit tight. You can get up and move around if you like, but I need everyone to stay on the bus."

"Can we put another movie in?" asked Trevor.

"Mrs. Park's in charge of that now," Mr. Dante said. "But it's fine with me." He handed Mrs. Park a stack of movie cases, then followed the driver off the bus.

"Wish we had *House of the Wicked*," I told Owen, sighing. "It'd be perfect right now."

"Probably better than what we're about to watch." Owen pointed to the case Mrs. Park was opening.

I groaned. "*Seven Dates*? Ugh."

While Owen pulled out his video game, I turned around in my seat and scanned the seats. In the very back, I spotted black, curly hair. Julia's head was tilted to the side, headphones on, eyes closed. Several rows in front of her, Aaron leaned out in the aisle to talk to Liam. Natasha sat next to him, slumped against the window.

"I'm going to go talk to Natasha for a while," I told Owen. "Maybe more Warlock later?"

"Okay!"

A few seconds later, I slid into the empty seat in front of Natasha, shifting so that I could see her between the window and my chair. "Hi!"

She perked up. "Hey! Glad you're here, I'm bored."

"Yeah," I said, glancing pointedly up at the TV over our heads. "This could totally put you into a coma."

Natasha laughed. "You *know* I love this movie, Holly! Even you said it wasn't that bad when Julia and I finally got you to come see it with us last year."

"I never said that," I told her. "I said I didn't have a bad time. Because I took such a nice nap in the theater."

She rolled her eyes. "Weirdo. Hey, do you think now would be a good time to go talk to Julia?"

Leaning closer, I lowered my voice. "Probably not. Apparently, she's been griping about us to Sophie."

"What?"

I told Natasha everything Leah had said. When I finished, she was frowning.

"We didn't *yell* at her!" she said. "She's the one who yelled at us!"

"I know." I picked at a small hole in the side of my chair. "I don't want to fight with Julia, but . . . I can't believe she's so mad at us. Like we're supposed to just be okay with her ditching us for Seth all the time, or not showing up to her own surprise party."

"So what should we do?" Natasha asked. "If we try to talk to her, we'll probably just end up fighting again."

"Yeah. Maybe we should just leave her alone for a while." I sighed. "Although that's going to be hard to do once we're all in the hotel room."

"You mean the party room?" Gabby's head popped up over the back of Natasha's chair, a Twizzler sticking out of her mouth like a cigar.

"I don't know about that," Natasha told her. "Things are kind of weird between us and Julia right now."

"But she can't stay mad at us," I added, even though I wasn't so sure. "Not when we're all sharing a room, right?"

"Ah, man." Gabby bit off the end of the Twizzler. "So she hasn't told you guys yet."

"Told us what?" I sat up straight.

"Well . . ." Gabby leaned closer. "Julia swapped with Victoria, so Victoria's in our room instead. I guess Julia asked Mrs. Park about it during lunch."

"She switched rooms?" I cried, then clapped my hand over my mouth and glanced around. Aaron was still talking to Liam, but I lowered my voice just in case. "I can't believe she did that without even talking to us about it!"

"What's the deal, anyway?" Gabby asked. "Is this about her not showing up to the party Saturday?"

Natasha and I filled her in on everything, from the nonstop Seth-talk to our conversation with Julia yesterday.

"So it wasn't just the party, you know?" I accepted a Twizzler even though my stomach was all knotted up again. "That was just sort of the last straw. She's been doing stuff like that ever since we got back from winter break, and it's only getting worse."

"And when we tried to explain that to her, she made it seem like we were just trying to make her feel guilty about the party," Natasha said. "She got really defensive."

Gabby nodded slowly. "Well, maybe she felt like you guys were ganging up on her."

"We weren't!" I exclaimed. "That's not what you think, is it? It's not like we just started yelling at her. We—"

"I know you didn't," Gabby interrupted. "I'm just

saying . . ." She stopped, making a face. "I don't know. I guess I'm saying Seth is her first boyfriend, so I bet she had no idea she was talking about him so much, or making you feel left out. She probably *did* feel bad, but I bet she was kind of embarrassed, too."

I pictured Julia in the cubby room, her eyes all red and watery. "I guess so," I said, and I could tell from Natasha's expression that she felt as guilty as I did. "But that's no reason to yell at us, is it?"

"What were we supposed to do?" Natasha added. "Just say nothing while she keeps ditching us for Seth?"

Shrugging, Gabby rested her chin on the back of Natasha's seat. "No. But if you try to talk to her while she's still mad, and *you're* still mad, you'll just end up fighting more." She gave me a pointed look. "And unless you've got mad ninja skills like in that freaky cyborg movie you made us watch, I don't want to see any fighting." Stretching her arm over Natasha's head, Gabby tried to stick her Twizzler up my nose. I swatted her hand away, laughing despite myself.

"No fighting, I promise."

I chewed my Twizzler (*not* the one that had almost been in my nostril) while Gabby made fun of *Seven Dates*, and Natasha pretended to be offended. But my thoughts kept straying back to Julia. Gabby was right—if I tried to talk to her now, when we were both upset, it would probably lead to a fight.

Still . . . I peered at the front of the bus and saw Mr. Dante on his cell phone. Mrs. Park stood next to him, listening. Judging from the looks on their faces, the mechanic hadn't given them good news.

The whole band was stuck on a broken-down bus in the middle of nowhere. Maybe we'd sleep on the bus, or camp out in a field. Either way, this trip was about to get seriously interesting, and I didn't want to spend it ignoring my best friend.

First chance I got, I was going to talk to Julia and straighten this whole mess out.

It turned out "broken engine" also meant "no air conditioning or movies." The mechanic called for a tow truck, but it was two towns over, so they said we'd have to wait at least an hour. Mr. Dante tried to get a local school bus to take us someplace to hang out, but since it was almost three o'clock, all the district's buses were taking kids home from school. And we couldn't even go outside because Mr. Dante and the chaperones said there wasn't enough room between the fence and the road for us to stand safely. Natasha and I pressed our faces to the window, but highway, fences, and farmland extended out in both directions as far as we could see.

Forty-two kids, five chaperones, and one band director stuck in a bus with no air conditioning in eighty-something-degree weather. Things got real gross, real fast.

"Trevor, I swear to *Zeus*," Gabby yelled, pinching

her nose and making her voice all nasally. "If you don't put your shoes back on, I am literally going to sue you."

Trevor snorted without looking up from his video game. He was leaning against his window in the seat in front of Gabby, his bare feet dangling in the aisle. "Sue me for what?"

"For—for polluting the air," Gabby announced. "I'm choking to death over here."

For a few seconds, Trevor didn't respond. Then, slowly, his foot appeared over the top of his seat. Gabby glanced up a second too late, shrieking at the sight of his toes inches away from her nose. Natasha and I laughed as she scrambled out of her chair and hurried to the back of the bus.

"It *is* getting pretty ripe in here," Natasha said, fanning her face with her music folder. I nodded in agreement. My hair was a humidity nightmare—half sweaty and plastered to my forehead and neck, half frizzed out in all directions. But everyone looked so grungy, I didn't feel too self-conscious.

Aaron still somehow managed to look good, of course. (Not that I was staring or anything.) He'd spent most of the last hour talking to Liam and Gabe across the aisle, even though he was still sitting next to Natasha. It was kind of weird. They weren't ignoring each other exactly—they still joked around a little and smiled at each other and stuff—but really, what's the point of sitting with your boyfriend or girlfriend if you're going to spend more time talking to everybody else?

Maybe that was partly my fault for coming to sit in front of Natasha. But apparently she'd spent most of the ride before we broke down trading fashion magazines back and forth with Victoria, who sat two rows behind her. I flipped through one for a few minutes, but it was from last fall and looking at all the winter furs and boots made me feel ten times hotter. Leaning against the window, I fanned the back of my neck with the magazine and squinted down the highway at something yellow on the horizon.

"Hey, a school bus!" I cried, sitting up. "Do you think it's for us?"

Natasha leaned over to look. "Is it empty? *Please* let it be empty . . ."

I crossed my fingers as the bus got closer, then blinked when someone shoved a few bottles of aerosol body spray in my face.

"Sweet Pea or Vanilla Sugar—which one smells girlier?" asked Gabby, shaking the bottles. I wrinkled my nose.

"I don't know, but are you sure you want to use that now?" I asked. "It's so gross in here, they'll just make the smell worse."

Gabby studied the bottles. "Yeah, you're right," she said, nodding. "I should use both."

"That's not what I said!"

But Gabby was moving up the aisle again before I'd even finished the sentence. Crouching like a cat behind

Trevor's seat, she shook both bottles hard. Then she pounced.

"*Auughhhhhh!*" Trevor flailed his arms wildly, his video game flying through the air as Gabby sprayed him. "*Quit it quit it quit it!*"

"*Cover up your stinky feet!*" Gabby hollered, chasing him a few steps down the aisle until Mrs. Park grabbed the bottles out of her hands. Trevor fled to the back and locked himself in the bathroom while everyone laughed. (Well, and gagged. Vanilla and sweat weren't exactly complementary aromas.)

"Gabby, I think we need to have a little chat," Mrs. Park said sternly, and Gabby sighed.

"Sorry, but his feet are lethal weapons. I had to defend myself."

I couldn't help giggling, even though poor Mrs. Park looked like she was beginning to regret signing up to be a chaperone. Before she could start lecturing Gabby, the doors opened and Mr. Dante stepped back onto the bus. He opened his mouth, but apparently the smell hit him before he could get a word out, because he made such a funny face everyone started cracking up again.

"Ms. Flores, did the candy factory in your backpack explode?"

Gabby grinned. "Nah. Although I had a bag of chocolate bars that melted. Now it looks like a bag of p—"

"That's enough," Mr. Dante interrupted, shaking his head. "Okay, everyone—take what you'll need for the next few hours. The tow truck will be here soon, and we've got another bus waiting to take us someplace to hang out until ours is fixed."

There was a mad scramble to get off the bus and away from the vanilla-sweat smell, which seemed to get stronger every second in the heat. The school bus wasn't any cooler, but at least it didn't stink. (Well, unless you sat close to Trevor. Which only Owen was nice enough to do.)

We ended up spending three hours at a burger place playing Warlock while the mechanic worked on the bus. In the end, he said it wouldn't be ready until tomorrow. And, Mr. Dante informed us, there were no hotels nearby with enough rooms available.

"Stranded!" I exclaimed, throwing my cards down on the table. "So are we going to sleep in an abandoned barn? Or camp out near a cornfield that's a secret hideout for zombies? Or maybe there's an old haunted house or a—"

"Holly." Mr. Dante cut me off and waited for everyone at my table to stop giggling. "I've made a few phone calls, and there's a school about a mile from here on the way to the shop."

"A haunted school?" I asked hopefully, but he shook his head.

"The principal is going to open the gym," he went on. "She's already started asking around for people to donate pillows and blankets. We'll have access to the bathrooms and the vending machines."

"We're going to sleep in the gym?" Gabby asked, her eyes wide.

Mr. Dante nodded. "Should be okay for one night, right?"

"Okay?" she cried. "This is *awesome*!"

Judging by the excited chatter that followed, everyone agreed. Well, except for the chaperones. I saw Mrs. Park swallow a few aspirin before throwing her soda away and herding us back onto the bus.

The school turned out to be an elementary, middle, *and* high school all in one building—and it was still way smaller than Millican. The gym was tiny. I was pretty sure it was less than half the size of that crazy-huge band hall at Bishop.

A lot of locals turned up with sleeping bags and stuff for us. One woman even brought cookies from her bakery. The chaperones spread the blankets and pillows out all over the gym floor, but we ended up clustered together in the middle. By nine o'clock, we had the biggest game of Warlock *ever* going on. More than half the band was playing—even Aaron and Natasha joined in.

"Lights out in one hour," Mr. Dante told us. "We've got to get an early start tomorrow morning if we still want to visit the zoo before rehearsal."

"When you say lights out, do you mean 'lights out so we can tell ghost stories'?" Victoria asked innocently, swiping one of Max's cards.

Mr. Dante smiled. "Nope, sorry. Although I'm sure Holly knows some good ones," he added before heading back over to the chaperones. Gabby pointed her cards at me.

"Ghost story," she ordered. "Go."

Before I could respond, Aaron spoke up. "No, I want to hear about the zombie cornfield movie you mentioned earlier. What's it called?"

"*Zombie Farmers*," I said, taking Trevor's swamp demon. "I thought it was going to be gory, but it turned out to be more like a comedy."

Liam glanced up from his cards. "Oh, I wanted to see that. It's not gory?" He sounded disappointed.

"Well, it kind of is," I said.

Owen looked like he was trying not to laugh. "What do you mean by *kind of*?"

I shrugged. "Well, it's a zombie movie. It's got some gross stuff. But mostly it's kind of funny. The zombies are trying to live normal lives as farmers—they eat beets instead of brains. But anytime they go into town just to buy milk or whatever, the townspeople freak out and think they're being attacked. Probably because the zombies are always covered in beet juice and it kinda looks like blood. So the townspeople decide they're going to destroy the zombies' farm."

"How?" asked Aaron.

Realizing I had everyone's attention, I sat up a little straighter. "First, a bunch of them break into the zombies' cellar. They panic because they see all these jars filled with what they think are eyeballs, but it's really just pickled radishes. They try to set fire to the farmhouse, but one of the zombies finds them and they run off screaming when he tries to offer them some raspberry iced tea . . ."

We kept the game going while I described most of the movie. It was pretty fun, with everyone yelling *ew* or laughing in all the right places. But when I got to the part where the townspeople are sneaking through the cornfields at night and they don't notice that the scarecrows are actually the zombies in disguise, I noticed Natasha's face. She looked genuinely freaked out, and no one—including Aaron—seemed to notice.

"I need a drink," I announced, setting my cards down. "Natasha, want to come?"

She gave me a relieved smile and nodded.

"What about the ending?" Aaron asked. "What happens?"

"You'll just have to watch it sometime," I told him with a grin.

Natasha and I walked across the gym together. "Thanks for doing that," she said as soon as we were a safe distance from the group.

"Doing what?"

"You know," Natasha said. "Stopping the horror talk. I know you probably think I'm being stupid, but I don't know . . . that stuff really creeps me out."

"I don't think you're being stupid. I'm really sorry,"

I told her, and I meant it. I felt bad about how scared she'd looked. "I guess I got carried away."

"It's okay."

The doors opened just as we reached them. "Oh! Hi, girls," said Mrs. Park, stepping back to let us out of the gym. "Where are you headed?"

"Just to the water fountain," I replied.

"Right around the corner." Mrs. Park lowered her voice. "And could you do me a favor?"

"Sure!"

"Would you check on Julia?" she asked. "She asked to use the restroom a while ago, and I think she's still in there. I just want to make sure she's okay."

Natasha and I exchanged an uneasy glance. "No problem," I said. As soon as we turned the corner, Natasha grabbed my hand.

"You don't think a zombie farmer got her, do you?" She sounded only half-joking, but I couldn't help giggling.

"Doubt it." Then I stopped, tugging Natasha's arm and pointing. "Look." Near the end of the hall, someone was leaning against the lockers. The light from the cell phone in her hands was just bright enough for me to make out Julia's face.

Natasha sighed. "Gee, I wonder who she's calling."

"Yeah." I headed to the water fountain and took a long drink, then waited while Natasha did the same. "So?" I asked when she finished.

"So . . . what?"

"Should we go talk to her?"

Frowning, Natasha turned to squint down the hall again. Julia was pacing back and forth, still staring at her phone. "I don't know. I thought we were going to leave her alone for a while."

"I know, but this is ridiculous," I said. "I don't want to spend this trip fighting with Julia. Do you?"

"Of course not!"

"Okay then." I linked my arm with hers. "Let's go."

When we got about halfway down the hall, Julia glanced up and saw us. She froze, eyeing us warily.

"Hey." I smiled at her.

Julia looked from me to Natasha. "Hey," she said quietly.

So far, so good. "Julia," I started. "We really want to talk to you about—"

A strange, tinny sound cut me off, startling all of us. Julia stared down at her cell phone. *New ringtone*, I thought, and after a second, I recognized it—her favorite Infinite Crush song.

"It's Seth." Julia winced, as if she hadn't meant to say his name out loud.

I kept my voice light. "Could you call him back in a few minutes? We—"

"I've been trying to get reception for, like, half an hour," Julia said, and without waiting for either of us to respond, she tapped the screen and held it to her ear. "Hi! Hang on a sec, okay?" Cupping the bottom of the phone, she glanced at me. "Can we talk later?"

Second place again. I rolled my eyes, the irritation I'd felt earlier returning full force. "Yeah. Later."

Julia's expression hardened. Without another word, she turned her back on us and walked to the very end of the corridor.

Natasha looked as defeated as I felt. "Well, that went well."

"Yup."

We headed back to the gym, Julia's whispered conversation growing fainter with each step.

I didn't see Julia come back to the gym, but when the chaperones woke us up early the next morning, she was curled up in a sleeping bag near the wall. And by "the chaperones woke us up," I really meant "Mrs. Park blasted some sort of air horn that scared everyone to death."

"Got it at that shop next to the taco place yesterday," she told the other parents with a big smile. "I might have to start using this at home."

Not far from where they stood, Liam groaned and rubbed his eyes. "Great."

We folded and stacked the blankets and sleeping bags in groggy silence. After washing up in the gym restrooms (fun as this was, I couldn't *wait* for the hotel room and a real shower) we piled back onto the bus. Mr. Dante laughed when he saw us.

"Not really morning people, are you?" he asked. I glanced around. We did look pretty rough, although some more than others. It looked like Trevor had somehow managed to get from the gym to the bus without opening his eyes. He fell into the seats behind me and Owen with an exaggerated moan. I could've sworn he still smelled a little bit like Gabby's vanilla and sweet pea body sprays.

We were all so tired, no one even asked to put in a movie. My eyes felt heavy and gritty. Even after everyone had finally gone to sleep last night, I couldn't stop thinking about Julia. It was a weird feeling, missing her and being angry at her at the same time. I didn't know how to fix this. For a while, I'd tried to direct my anger at Seth, but I couldn't. It wasn't his fault Julia liked hanging out with him more than her friends. So then I'd tried to convince myself that this was just what happened when boyfriends came into the picture . . . but that wasn't true, either. Natasha had been dating Aaron just as long, and if anything, she and I were closer than ever.

It had taken forever to fall asleep. When Mrs. Park had started blasting that air horn, I felt like I'd only been out for a few minutes.

"How long till New Orleans?" I asked Mr. Dante as the bus pulled out of the parking lot.

"About two hours."

Yawning, I glanced at Owen. He leaned against the window, backpack unopened at his feet. Shifting in my chair, I tried to find a position that would allow me to sleep without any danger of accidental cuddling.

Although to be totally honest, it was tempting. Sleeping on Owen's shoulder was comfortable. So sue me.

Better not risk freaking him out, though. I curled up in my chair, facing the aisle, and fell asleep. But it was one of those naps where you actually feel *more* tired afterward. My head kept falling forward, and I'd wake up with a start each time, then drift off again. By the time we got to the hotel, I had a severe crick in my neck and my left arm was numb.

Everyone else looked about as cranky as I felt. We unloaded our luggage from the compartment under the bus while Mr. Dante checked in, then waited while the chaperones handed out our room keys. I couldn't help but stare at Julia when Mrs. Park called her forward with Leah, Sophie, and Brooke, but she kept her eyes on her shoes.

Once we had our keys, I followed Natasha, Gabby, and Victoria into the elevator. Between all of our suitcases and instruments, it was kind of a tight squeeze.

"Hands out," Gabby ordered the second the elevator doors slid shut. She ripped open a massive bag of M&M's, and we obediently cupped our hands while she poured.

"Too many!" Natasha exclaimed, laughing when Gabby just kept pouring. When the three of us had overflowing handfuls of candy, Gabby held her finger over the button for the twelfth floor.

"You all need to wake up," she said sternly. "I'm not going to the zoo with a bunch of grumpy people who haven't had a real breakfast. And by breakfast, I mean sugar rush. So here's the deal—you've got until the elevator gets to our floor to eat everything in your hands. Ready? *Go.*"

Without waiting for a response, Gabby pressed the button, then tilted her head back and poured what was left in the bag into her mouth. Victoria immediately crammed her entire handful into her mouth, too, making her cheeks bulge like a chipmunk. Natasha and I cracked up.

"*Mmmshhph!*" Gabby pointed frantically at the buttons as we moved from the fourth floor to the fifth. I stuffed my M&M's into my mouth and turned away from Natasha—if we made eye contact, I'd start laughing again and probably choke.

When the elevator reached the twelfth floor, we were all still chewing except for Gabby.

"Amateurs." She grinned at us before dragging her suitcase down the hall. Victoria tapped my shoulder when we stopped in front of our room.

"Do I have something in my teeth?" Her mouth stretched into an enormous, chocolaty smile, and Gabby and I snickered.

"Ew!" Natasha cried. Two M&M's fell out of her mouth, which only made us laugh harder.

Gabby unlocked the door, and Natasha made a beeline for the bathroom. Victoria and I collapsed onto the beds, while Gabby went straight to the door connected to the room next to us. She knocked loudly, yelling, "Hey, neighbors!"

"Gabby!" I sat up, still giggling. "They might be total strangers!"

"Nah, it's—"

The door flew open, cutting Gabby off.

"I need food," Leah announced, stepping inside our room. Gabby opened her backpack and pulled out another enormous bag of M&M's.

"Here you go. Mrs. Park told me we were next to Leah's room," she added, glancing at me.

"Cool!" I smiled, trying to look unconcerned about the fact that Julia was right next door, possibly even gossiping to Sophie about what horrible friends Natasha and I were at this very moment. Despite the fact that we'd tried to talk to her to clear the whole thing up not once, but twice.

Maybe I was sick of worrying about it, or maybe it was the sugar rush kicking in. Either way, I was suddenly determined to have fun on this trip. With or without Julia.

Hopping off the bus at the zoo, I squinted at the overcast sky and zipped my hoodie. The air was chillier than yesterday, but still humid—I didn't need a mirror to know my hair was already frizzing up. I pulled a rubber band out of my pocket to tie it back, waiting for Owen.

"Your bag looks a lot lighter," I said when he came down the steps. Owen glanced at his backpack.

"Yeah, but our seats are kind of a mess," he said apologetically. "I ended up just dumping everything out except for my sketchbook and pencils."

I shrugged, glancing at the bus windows. "No big deal. We'll clean it up when we get back."

His eyes widened. "Did you just say *no big deal?*"

"Yeah. What?" I added, because he was still staring.

"Holly, you spent two hours alphabetizing my DVDs last semester," Owen said. "And every time you stay over for dinner, my mom jokes about hiring you to do the dishes because they end up cleaner than when she runs them through the dishwasher."

"What's your point?"

"My point is that our seats are covered in DVDs and snacks." He paused. "The box of crackers might have spilled a little, too. And you're not freaking out?"

Normally, the thought of cracker crumbs all over my chair would have made me cringe. But I'd just spotted Julia through the bus window, getting close to the front.

"So the crackers spilled," I said, grabbing Owen's hand and pulling him away from the bus. "No big deal, like I said. Come on!"

We hurried to the zoo entrance, where Mrs. Park was handing out tickets. "First ones here!" she said with a smile, checking us off her list. Inside, we passed a few short buildings and a fountain. After a good two minutes of walking, I suddenly realized I'd never let go of Owen's hand.

Okay. This was . . . interesting.

I didn't want to just drop it out of nowhere. That would be rude, right? But it was one of those things that once you noticed it, you couldn't *not* notice it. Like a giant spotlight was shining on our hands or something. It made me feel really self-conscious, but at the same time, I didn't necessarily want to let go. It was a confusing feeling.

I wondered if Owen had blinked his eyelids off yet. It's what he always did when he was confused.

Between this and the accidental cuddling on the bus, he'd probably set a blinking record by now.

Taking care to be as subtle as possible, I glanced at him. He looked . . . normal. No blushing, no blinking.

"The primate exhibit's over there," I said, pointing at the sign. "Want to check that out first?"

"Sure!" He sounded normal, too.

Huh. Maybe I was freaking out over nothing. Maybe holding hands really *wasn't* a big deal. (Unlike the spilled crackers on my seat, which made me twitch every time I pictured it.)

We walked to the railing and peered down. I spotted two gorillas right away, both sitting on the giant rocks in the middle of the grounds.

"Whoa," I said. "You've got to draw them."

"Definitely," Owen agreed. We let go of each other's hands at the same time, and he pulled his sketchbook and pencils out of his backpack. I felt relieved. Okay, 90 percent relieved and 10 percent disappointed.

"Hey, guys." Gabby appeared behind us, holding an enormous funnel cake.

"Hey!" I glanced around. Victoria and Leah were coming around the corner, but I didn't see anyone else from Millican. "Where is everybody, anyway?"

"Mostly in the food court," she replied. "Victoria said something about going to see the sea lions first. Wanna come?"

"Maybe when Owen finishes." I pointed at his sketchbook, and Gabby leaned over to look.

"*Wow*." She shook her head. "Geez, Owen. That's amazing."

He smiled, face flushed, pencil still flying. "Thanks."

After Gabby followed Victoria and Leah down the path to the sea lion exhibit, I watched Owen draw. My eyes flickered back and forth between the sketch-gorillas and the real ones. Yeah, he was definitely getting better. He'd even captured their facial expressions. It sounded kind of silly, but it was like you could see their personalities somehow.

When he finished with the gorillas, we headed to the sea lions. I spotted Max and Trevor, but Gabby and the others were gone. Owen and I ended up wandering around kind of aimlessly, talking about our Alien Park science fair project. Being at the zoo was giving us all sorts of new ideas—by the time we got to the swamp, we had a list of ten alien exhibits.

A crowd had gathered on the boardwalk. Owen and I joined them, standing on our toes and peering around heads. The swamp had a funny smell, like shrimp and dirty socks.

"Can you see?" I asked him.

"No . . . oh, I think they're feeding the alligators!"

We managed to squeeze through to the front just in time. A zookeeper stood at the edge of the grass, holding a long pole out over the greenish water. Something pink was stuck on the end of the pole.

"A raw chicken," I said. "Awesome."

Owen laughed. When the first alligator swam up

to the bank, several people shrieked. The zookeeper kept a safe distance, waving the chicken over its head. The alligator froze, eyeing the pole, then—*snap!*—it snatched the chicken in its jaws. For a few seconds the alligator and the zookeeper wrestled with the pole, like the world's most dangerous game of tug-of-war. Then the alligator disappeared back under the murk, leaving the zookeeper with a chicken-free pole.

I looked at Owen. "So . . . we should have an alien feeding exhibit, right?"

"*Yes*." He added it to the list.

We left the boardwalk and headed into a small, dark building. Two older girls left through the exit on the other side, leaving us alone. It took a few seconds for my eyes to adjust after the door closed. Tanks of all sizes lined one wall, all filled with snakes and lizards. The other side was a glass wall—behind that there was an elevated habitat with a lot of rocks, a small cave, and a pond that ended at the glass, so you could see under the surface of the water.

"Whoa!" I exclaimed, stepping up to the glass. Three white alligators lay perfectly still on the rocks. I thought they were fake at first—marble or something. But then one scrambled away from the others, slipping into the pond. The way it glided through the water was so graceful.

"Ghosts." Mesmerized, I watched it paddle right past us. "They're like ghost alligators."

Owen looked at me for a second. Then he turned

and sat on the floor against the wall with all the snakes, right across from the habitat. Pulling out his sketchbook, he began scribbling furiously. I was still gazing at the alligators a few minutes later when my cell phone beeped with a text. Natasha.

Where are you?

Reptile house, I texted back, then joined Owen on the floor. He paused when I leaned over to look, his hand still covering the right side of the sketch.

My mouth fell open. It was the habitat—the rocks, the cave, the pond. But instead of three alligators, there were seven or eight. And instead of swimming, they were *flying*. Soaring in the air, plunging into the water . . . two looked like they were doing flips.

Something else was different, too. I leaned closer, squinting in the dim light. The alligators' edges were blurred, like Owen had smudged them on purpose. One floated on its side past a large rock, belly facing out, and I could see the rock *through* it. Somehow, he'd drawn the alligators to look transparent.

"Ghost alligators," Owen explained. He sounded uncertain, I guess because I hadn't said anything. "Do you like it?"

Finally, I tore my eyes off the picture and looked at him. "That is . . ." I paused, because *awesome* or *amazing* didn't seem like big enough compliments. "It's my favorite," I said at last. "Of all your drawings. Ever."

Owen smiled. "Thanks, Holly."

Suddenly, I was very aware of how close we were

sitting. Pretty much shoulder-to-shoulder. Which was my fault—I'd leaned in too close to look at the drawing. He didn't seem to mind, though.

We both glanced up when the door opened. I shaded my eyes from the daylight streaming inside.

"Holly?" Natasha called. "Are you in here?"

"Over here!" I shifted away from Owen a little bit.

The door closed, and Natasha shuffled toward us. "What are you guys do—" she started. Then she noticed the white alligator gliding past the glass and let out a little shriek. "That thing is creepy!"

I grinned. "You think everything's creepy."

Rolling her eyes, Natasha sunk down to the floor next to me. "Alligators *are* creepy. Did you see that crazy guy feeding them chickens? They could bite his arm off!"

Laughing, Owen returned to his sketch. I glanced at the door before turning to Natasha. "So why are you wandering around by yourself?"

She shrugged. "Aaron and some of the others are still out there watching them feed the alligators, but . . . you know. Ew."

I watched Natasha fiddle with her shoelaces. Her expression was kind of funny, like she wanted to say something, but didn't want to at the same time. And just when I opened my mouth to ask her what was wrong, she blurted it out.

"I think I'm going to break up with him."

She kept her eyes on her laces. On my other side,

for just a second or so, Owen's pencil went completely still. I guess Natasha noticed, too, because she laughed a little.

"Sorry, Owen. You probably don't want to hear about this."

I glanced at him and caught a few blinks. "It's okay," he said without looking up.

"You won't tell anyone, right?" she added.

"No!"

"Thanks." Natasha waited a moment, then nudged my arm. "Well? No comment?"

I cleared my throat. "Sorry. Um . . . what happened? Did you have a fight or something?"

"No, nothing like that! It's just . . ." She stopped, wrinkling her nose. "I don't know. He's really nice, and the first few times we went out, it was a lot of fun. But we just don't have a lot in common, you know? Like at lunch—I never know what to say when I'm around his friends. Honestly, most of the time I just wish I was sitting with you guys instead. Or like that one time I told you about, when I ended up talking to his mom in the kitchen because him and his friends were all watching one of your creepy movies," she added with a teasing grin. "Why do you keep lending him those, anyway?"

She didn't look upset at all, but I felt horrible. "I'm really sorry," I started, but she cut me off.

"I'm just joking, Holly!"

"Really?" I asked. I couldn't stop picturing her face

in the gym last night when I was talking about the zombie farmers.

But Natasha was giggling. "Of course, *really*. You both like the same gross movies, that doesn't bother me." She sighed. "The movies are just one example, anyway. To be honest, I bet he's probably thinking about breaking up with me, too. We're just running out of things to talk about."

"Oh." I didn't know what to say. "I'm really sorry. Are you okay?"

"Yeah." Natasha made a face. "Well, I'm okay with everything except the actual conversation. I mean, what should I say?"

I tried to think of something helpful, then sighed. "I have no idea. I guess . . . I guess you should just tell him what you told me. You like him, but you don't have much in common, and you still want to be friends."

Natasha made a noise that was half-laugh, half-groan. "It sounds so easy when you put it that way, but when I think about actually saying it to his face . . . ugh."

"Sorry," I said again. "But hey—if you tell him while he's still watching the alligator feeding and one *does* bite that guy's arm off, maybe your breaking up with him won't seem so bad in comparison."

Natasha tried to look disgusted, but ended up laughing instead. "You're so weird, Holly."

"Thanks." I smiled at her. "Hey, did you eat lunch yet?"

"Nope, unless you count the M&M's."

I looked at Owen, whose pencil was still flying away. "Want to go get some food?"

"Sure." He flipped the sketchbook closed.

"Did you finish it?" I asked him as we stood up. "The ghost alligators?"

"Not yet," Owen replied, zipping his backpack. His voice sounded funny, kind of like he was nervous or something. "I'll work on it more later."

"Oh my God, they *do* look like ghost alligators," Natasha said. "I'm so going to have nightmares about those things." Covering her eyes with her hands, she started walking blindly to the door.

"Don't look to your left," I called after her. "That rattlesnake's cage doesn't look too sturdy."

"Shut *up*!" Natasha yelled. I laughed, and Owen did, too. We followed Natasha out of the reptile house, squinting in the bright light.

"So can I see the ghost alligator drawing when it's finished?" I asked, glancing at Owen.

"Um . . . yeah." He gave me a quick smile. "Sure."

"Thanks."

All of Natasha's break-up talk must have weirded him out, I realized. My good mood was fading, too, although that could've been because my sugar rush was finally wearing off. It got worse when we passed Julia, sitting alone on a bench and texting. She didn't even look up.

So far, this trip was not going the way I'd expected. Julia would rather talk on the phone with Seth than hang out with us. Natasha and Aaron were breaking up. And Owen and I had walked around holding hands like it wasn't a big deal.

Band trips, I decided, did weird things to relationships.

When we got back to the hotel from the zoo, Mr. Dante gave us an hour to get ready for dinner. An *hour.* As if that could possibly be enough time for four girls sharing one bathroom.

We barely made it downstairs on time. And while Mrs. Park did a head count in the lobby, Trevor and a few other kids realized they'd left their instruments upstairs, even though Mr. Dante had reminded us at least a dozen times that we had rehearsal after dinner. So by the time the bus pulled out of the parking lot, we were way behind schedule.

Max and Victoria found a big, round table in the back of the restaurant. After going through the buffet line, Owen, Trevor, and I joined them. We'd been playing Warlock for a few minutes, sliding cards in between baskets of fried shrimp and hush puppies, when Natasha sat down next to me.

I glanced up in surprise. "Hey!"

"Hi." She grinned when she saw the cards. "You guys are obsessed."

"Want to play?" Max offered her a stack, but Natasha shook her head.

"Not right now, thanks."

I waited until no one was paying attention before leaning closer to her. "Did you do it?"

"No, not yet." Natasha sighed, picking at her fries. "Too many people around, you know? I don't want to tell him in front of Liam—or anyone, for that matter."

"Yeah." I tossed a shield-spell card onto the stack in the middle of the table. "It's not like there's a lot of privacy on the bus. Maybe you should wait until after the trip."

She made a face. "Maybe . . . but now that I know I'm going to do it, I just want to get it over with."

I nodded. "Rip off the Band-Aid."

"Exactly."

But Natasha was right about the lack of privacy. After dinner, we boarded the bus again and headed straight to the college campus hosting the contest. Rehearsal got off to a shaky start—after all, we hadn't practiced since Monday. And between sleeping on the gym floor last night and a whole day out at the zoo, everyone was starting to look kind of wrecked. Even the big box of Red Hots Gabby had shared after dinner wasn't working.

It didn't help that I was sitting last chair, too. Not because I was upset about it—although after making all-region, it *was* sort of embarrassing that I'd messed up that chair test so badly. I knew I'd do better on the next one, though. And in the meantime, I got to sit next to Owen, since he was third chair. But I was used to having the saxophones next to me on the right. Now, the second row of clarinets sat to my left. And my chair was more in front of the trombones than the trumpets. Our songs sounded different since I wasn't used to hearing those parts so loudly. It was kind of neat, but it threw me off a little.

Plus, Julia was only two chairs away in the row in front of me. I couldn't help glancing at her during rehearsal. It dawned on me that I hadn't seen her hanging out with anyone on the trip. Sure, she sat with Sophie on the bus. But in the gym, and at the zoo, she'd been alone.

Well, not alone, I reminded myself. *She has her phone, after all.* It was a mean thought, but it was true. And it helped me feel less bad. Because the truth was, phone or no phone, Julia looked pretty lonely.

"We have to be in the lobby at seven tomorrow morning," Owen said, reading his schedule while everyone packed up. "I might ask Mrs. Park for that air horn. Make sure Trevor actually gets up."

I laughed, but before I could respond, someone spoke up behind me.

"Hey, Holly?"

Turning, I found myself face-to-face with Aaron. For a second, I panicked—did he want to talk to me about Natasha? He'd asked me for advice last semester because she'd avoided him after the winter dance. It was nice that Aaron considered me a friend, but I so did *not* want to talk to him about their break-up.

"Yeah?" I said, stomach twisting with nerves.

"Want to run through the trio with me and Liam?" Aaron asked. "It's been a while, and Mr. Dante said the ensembles have half an hour before the bus leaves to practice."

"Oh!" I couldn't keep the relief out of my voice. "Yes, definitely."

"Cool," he replied. "Liam's in one of the practice rooms over there. I'm gonna go grab a drink first. Do you want anything?"

"No, thanks," I said. "I'll be there in a minute." Turning, I grabbed my folder and horn case. Owen was still staring at his schedule. "Guess I'll see you on the bus?" I asked. He nodded without looking up.

"Okay."

𝄞

Mrs. Park gave us a ten o'clock lights-out curfew. Like that was going to happen. Especially not when the room includes a girl with a seemingly endless supply of candy.

"Seriously, how much junk food did you pack?" I asked when Gabby pulled yet another package of Twizzlers from her bag.

"Oh, I went through everything I packed on the bus

yesterday," she replied. "But I stock up every time we stop at a gas station." Tossing me a few Twizzlers, Gabby headed for the door to the adjoining room. "We're going to play truth or dare. Wanna come?"

"I'll wait for Natasha."

Once Gabby and Victoria had joined the others next door, I stretched out on one of the beds. By the time Natasha got out of the shower, I'd dozed off with a Twizzler hanging out of my mouth.

Natasha poked me in the side, giggling. "Lucky for you I'm so nice. My camera's right there, and this would make a *great* picture."

Rubbing my eyes, I sat up. The Twizzler fell into my lap. "Ugh, I didn't realize I was so tired."

"Where are the others?" Natasha asked, settling onto the bed next to me.

"Next door. I told Gabby we'd go, too, but . . ."

"But Julia's over there," she finished.

"Yeah."

"Yeah." Natasha glanced at me. "So . . . how was practice? I mean, the trio?"

"Good," I said. "And Aaron didn't say anything to me about . . . you know. About you and him."

She laughed. "How'd you know that's what I wanted to ask?"

"Because I would've asked you the same thing," I told her, smiling.

The door opened, and Sophie stuck her head in. "Have you guys seen Julia?" she asked.

"Um . . . no," I said. "She's not in there with you?"

"Nope." Frowning, Sophie checked her watch. "She said she was going to get a drink, but that was a while ago. I'll go check the hall."

"Okay." I waited until Sophie had left before adding: "Ten bucks says she's on the phone with Seth again."

It came out angrier than I intended. Natasha glanced at me. "You okay?"

"Yes." I bit off another piece of Twizzler. "No, I'm not. It just really bothers me that Julia told Sophie about our fight. *Sophie*, of all people."

Natasha tilted her head. "What do you mean?"

"Because she's such a gossip!" I exclaimed. "Julia told her we yelled at her for hanging out with her boyfriend too much. It's like she did it because she knew Sophie would tell everyone, and they'd all think you and I were being mean."

"Oh." Natasha was quiet for a second. "No . . . I don't think that's why she talked to Sophie."

I looked at her in surprise. "What?"

"It's just . . ." Natasha cleared her throat. "Well, you're right—Sophie kind of is a gossip. But there's a reason she always knows everything about everyone. She's a really good listener."

"She is?" I shrugged. "Oh. I guess I don't know her that well."

"Yeah, she's actually pretty nice," Natasha said. "She and I talked a lot last semester when . . . um, when you and I . . ."

After a few seconds, I realized what she meant and laughed. "When we hated each other?"

Natasha giggled, too, her face pink. "Yeah. That." She grabbed one of my Twizzlers and bit off a small piece. "Anyway, I couldn't talk to Julia about it, so I talked to Sophie. I mean, not about *you*! Well, sort of about you. How we didn't like each other, and it was upsetting Julia, and I didn't know what to do. I was lonely, and I just wanted someone to talk to . . ." She trailed off, giving me a worried look.

I grinned. "It's okay, I know what you mean. That's part of why I ended up hanging out with Owen so much."

"Right." Natasha smiled back. "Well, I guess my point is that Sophie is easy to talk to. And her and Julia are in the same ensemble, remember? So they probably got to know each other a little better during all those practices, too."

A loud knock startled both of us. Natasha hopped off the bed and hurried to open the door.

"All right, girls," Mrs. Park said, stepping inside. "It's almost eleven, and we've got an early morning. Time to—" She stopped, looking around. "Where are your roommates?"

"Next door." Natasha stuck her head into Leah's room. "Gabby! Victoria! Mrs. Park's here."

After Mrs. Park went over tomorrow's schedule (and threatened to use her air horn to wake us up if necessary), she headed into the other room. As soon as the door closed, I turned to Gabby.

"Hey, did Sophie find Julia?"

"Yeah." Unzipping her suitcase, Gabby pulled out her pajamas. "She was in the lobby, but she came back up with Sophie. Lucky for her—we were supposed to be in our rooms by ten."

I shook my head. "Guess talking to Seth again was worth risking getting in trouble."

"I guess," Gabby said. "Something was definitely up, though. Her eyes were kind of red when she got back. I'm pretty sure she'd been crying."

Natasha and I exchanged worried looks. Maybe it was time to try talking to Julia again.

If I hadn't been so exhausted the next morning, I would've laughed when I got to the lobby. Everyone looked dead tired, even Mr. Dante. We were like zombies. A zombie band wearing really cool T-shirts.

The bus ride to the campus was only twenty minutes, but Trevor snored the whole way. "I don't know how you share a room with him," I told Owen.

"I've stayed over at his house plenty of times," he said with a shrug. "I came prepared."

"You mean you're used to it?"

Owen looked surprised. "No, I mean I brought earplugs."

My stomach tingled with nerves when we pulled into the parking lot. Mr. Dante had explained that this contest was like Solo and Ensemble—the judges would give us a rating based on our overall performance. He said it was good practice for the big contest we'd be attending in May. But thinking about this as just a practice performance wasn't helping me feel any less nervous about it. The concert hall would be open for anyone who wanted to watch, including students and parents from other schools.

Like all-region, I reminded myself. *And that went great, right? So just relax.*

It didn't work. I wondered how many performances it normally took before musicians stopped getting pre-concert jitters. Maybe I'd be over it by high school.

Warm-ups started kind of sluggish. But after we finished tuning, Mr. Dante blasted that air horn. Trevor yelled, "I'm awake, Mom!" and everyone laughed, and rehearsal ended up being really fun after that. I felt better by the time we filed onto the stage in the concert hall. The three judges were easy to spot, and the seats weren't even half full. Off to the side of the stage, I noticed a small cluster of chairs and music stands for the ensemble performances.

After Mr. Dante introduced us, we played our first song—a march we were also playing for the big contest at the end of the year. Then a few ensembles performed, including the quartet with Natasha, Gabe, Victoria, and Max.

After the band's second song, the percussion ensemble performed, followed by Julia's group. When they finished, I followed Aaron and Liam to the cluster of chairs and whispered "nice job" to Julia as she passed me. Surprise flickered across her face, but I thought I saw the trace of a smile, too.

"I can't find my music," Aaron said when I sat down. Liam and I just stared at him, and Aaron pulled his copy of "Triptych" out of his folder. "Just kidding," he added with a grin, and we snickered.

Tapping his foot, Aaron counted us off. Sitting in front of the whole band, not to mention the judges and everyone else in the concert hall, was a little intimidating. But it turned out to be the best we'd ever played the trio. By the time we finished, my cheeks were flushed and I felt a little giddy.

Pre-concert jitters, I decided, were totally worth the rush that came with a great performance. And apparently it was even more effective than Gabby's M&M sugar rush, because by the time we filed offstage, everyone was chatting and laughing and looking wide-awake. Out in the lobby, the chaperones herded us onto what looked like a choir's platform risers to take pictures.

"Stay with your sections!" Mrs. Park called, arranging the flute and clarinet players on the first row. "Saxes and French horns on the second row . . . Sophie, are you chewing gum? No, Trevor, please remove the hat."

Owen and I turned to see Trevor taking off a green cap with long ears like Yoda from *Star Wars* with a resigned sigh.

"Okay, folks," said the photographer once the chaperones made sure each section was holding their instruments the same way. "Stand up straight, look right here . . ." He wiggled his fingers over his head. "And . . . smile!"

Flash!

"All right, hang on just a minute and we'll do another one . . ." We rubbed our eyes while he adjusted his camera.

"We should switch places," Owen told me. "It's just a fluke that you're fourth chair. You shouldn't be positioned like this in the picture."

"It's not a fluke," I said. "You sounded better on the chair test than I did."

He shrugged. "Just that one time."

"You got a Superior rating on your solo, too," I reminded him. "It's pretty crazy that you're practicing so much with all the baseball stuff going on." He made kind of a funny face. "What?" I asked.

"Well . . ." Owen smiled a little. "That's kind of *why* I've been practicing more."

I stared at him for a second before realizing what he meant. "Because if you're practicing for band, Steve won't bug you to play baseball with him?"

"Yup."

The photographer spoke up again before I could say anything.

"Now let's try a fun one. Instruments on your head, goofy faces, whatever you want. You've got five seconds to strike a pose!"

"Can I wear my hat?" Trevor yelled, and Mrs. Park rolled her eyes.

"Why not."

Grinning, Trevor pulled the cap back on, then started swiping his trombone over me and Owen like a lightsaber. Laughing, we cowered with our hands over our heads just as the photographer snapped the shot.

"That'll be a good one," Owen said, and I grinned. Everyone kind of stampeded off the risers, and Owen tripped a little on the bottom step. I grabbed his hand and held it for a few seconds until we were safely on the ground. And then another second. And another. Because he wasn't letting go, and neither was I. Just when we were about to go from "helping each other off the platform" to "actually holding hands in front of the entire band," Mr. Dante called, "This way!" and we had to turn abruptly and follow him in the other direction.

I glanced at Owen. Okay, this time he was definitely a little pink-faced. Ugh, why did I keep doing this? Hopefully when we got back home, everything would go back to normal. Natasha caught my eye and smiled, and I wondered if she'd seen us. Well, better her than Gabby.

We filed down the hallway and stopped by the auditorium doors while Mr. Dante went inside. A few seconds later, he stepped out holding something behind his back with one hand and a sheet of paper with the other. He cleared his throat loudly, and everyone stopped talking.

"First of all, I want to tell you that I'm very proud of your performance," Mr. Dante began with a serious expression. Natasha and I exchanged nervous looks. It sounded like he was softening the blow of a really bad score. "I thought you did an outstanding job." He paused, smiling. "And apparently the judges agreed, because all three gave us a Superior rating!"

He held out a large gold trophy with purple and green sparkles, and everyone cheered. We headed back out to the parking lot, watching Trevor in his Yoda-cap wave the trophy over his head. Gabby skipped next to him, singing "We Are the Champions" at the top of her lungs.

"May the Force be with us!" Trevor swung the trophy through the air and accidentally swiped Mrs. Park's hair. Everyone laughed when she sighed and gently took the trophy from Trevor before he boarded the bus.

"Is it time to head home yet?" I overheard her say to Mr. Dante. She only sounded half-kidding.

Mr. Dante smiled. "I'm pretty sure the fun is only just beginning."

Chapter Seventeen

I figured I'd get to talk to Julia later that morning since we were going on a tour of the French Quarter. But as soon as we got on the bus, Mr. Dante told us we'd be grouped up with our roommates and a chaperone. So I ended up wandering through a cathedral with Natasha, Gabby, Victoria, and Mrs. Park. Thanks to Gabby's post-concert peanut butter cups, we were all hyper except for Mrs. Park. When we left the cathedral, squinting in the bright sunlight, she immediately pointed across the square.

"Coffee," she announced. "Let's go."

We followed her to a café with a huge pavilion and lots of tables. Mrs. Park stood in line while the four of us sat down.

"Victoria's going to kiss Max today," Gabby told us as soon as Mrs. Park was out of earshot. "It's her dare," she added when Natasha and I stared at her in confusion. "Truth or dare last night, remember? I dared her to."

I grinned at Victoria. "Are you really going to do it?"

"Probably," she said. "We—"

"Not *probably*," Gabby scolded. "That's not how truth or dare works."

Victoria rolled her eyes. "I should've just picked truth, but your truth questions are even worse than your dares."

"Yeah, but where's the fun in that, anyway?" Gabby asked. "I already knew you liked him."

"You do?" Smiling, Natasha turned to Victoria. "I didn't know that!"

Victoria grinned. "Yeah, we've been hanging out a lot lately. He asked me to the spring dance a few days ago. Hey," she added suddenly. "Do you want to go to dinner before the dance, like a double date? Him and Aaron are pretty good friends—it'd be fun!"

"Oh!" Natasha swallowed nervously. "Um, yeah, it would be. But . . . well, I don't think Aaron and I are going to the dance together."

"What?" Victoria's eyes widened. "Why not?"

"Well, don't tell anyone, but I'm going to break up with him."

I sat quietly while Natasha explained everything. A few times, I thought I caught Gabby glancing my way, but every time I looked back, her eyes were on Natasha.

"I'm really sorry," Victoria said when Natasha finished. "I understand, though. I went out with Liam a few times last semester. The first two times were fun, but by the third time, it was like suddenly we had nothing to talk about."

Natasha nodded. "Yeah, it's the same thing with us." She started to say something else, but stopped when Mrs. Park appeared with a huge tray. She set it down on our table—one coffee, four hot chocolates, and a few plates of what looked like mounds of powdered sugar.

Gabby's eyes bulged. "What is *that*?"

"Beignets," Mrs. Park replied. "They're like doughnuts. My treat, so help yourself!"

"I *love* you," Gabby said fervently, grabbing a beignet. She held it close to her nose, sniffed, and promptly sneezed. Powdered sugar flew everywhere, causing Natasha to shriek while Victoria and I burst out laughing. Unperturbed, Gabby shoved the entire beignet in her mouth. Her eyes fluttered closed.

"Thish ish shhhoo gooood," she murmured. Shaking her head, Mrs. Park took an extra-long sip of her coffee.

After devouring the beignets (which *were* amazing, although extremely messy), we walked around the square. It was close to noon, and it seemed like the crowd had doubled in the last half hour. Dozens of tables lined the curb, some displaying caricatures and paintings, others with tarot card readers and fortune-tellers. I stopped not far from one booth, which featured dozens of colorful sketches of dragons and castles. Owen would love them (although to be honest,

I thought his drawings were even better).

"Those are really cool," Gabby said, coming to stand next to me. "When I get a tattoo, it'll be a dragon." We giggled when Mrs. Park gave her a withering look. "What? Dragons are awesome. I want it to take up my whole back. Or maybe one like that," Gabby added, pointing to a purple, serpent-like dragon sketch. "I could get it wrapped around my arm!"

Mrs. Park drained her coffee and tossed it in the trash. "I'm not sure what your mother would think about that, Gabby."

"Oh, she already knows," Gabby assured her. "Tattoos don't bother her. She only gets worked up about stuff like how the cafeteria serves pizzas and burgers and not enough vegetables, or me hiding chocolate under my mattress." She paused, making a face. "That was the worst hiding spot ever. Everything melted—it was *so* hard to eat."

I was still laughing as Mrs. Park walked over to join Natasha and Victoria at a tarot booth. Gabby turned to face me, thumbs hooked in her pockets.

"So," she said, eyebrow raised.

"Um . . ." I blinked. "So what?"

"So, Natasha's breaking up with Aaron." Gabby poked my arm. "That's what. *So*, you know . . . he's single again."

"Wait," I said slowly. "Are you saying you think I should . . ."

"Ask him out?" Gabby lifted a shoulder. "I mean, obviously not right away. But maybe later, like to the spring dance? . . ." That could be fun.

I laughed. "No way."

"What if Natasha was okay with it, though?" she asked. "I mean, she doesn't seem too upset about breaking up with him. And there's still a few months till the dance. If you talked to her, I bet—"

"No, that's not it," I interrupted. "I don't want to ask Aaron out."

"You don't?" Gabby squinted at me, like she was trying to read my mind. "You don't like him anymore?"

"I like him," I said. "But I don't *like* him."

The funny thing was, I hadn't really thought about it until I said it. It was true, though. Aaron loved horror movies, and he was nice and funny and seriously disorganized. I liked being his friend. But I didn't have a crush on him. I really was over him.

"Well then, never mind," Gabby said with a grin. "Hey, maybe we can go stag again! Like we did for the winter dance."

I was saved from responding when Natasha and Victoria ran up to us, chatting excitedly about their tarot card reading. At some point, Gabby would find out I had a date to the dance already. She'd tease me relentlessly, which didn't bother me, but I knew she'd probably give Owen a hard time, too. I didn't want him to feel weird. And I *really* didn't want him to worry that I thought he had a crush on me, like last semester. The longer I could put off Gabby finding out that we were going to the spring dance together, the better.

Chapter Eighteen

My only mission during dinner that night was to find Julia. You wouldn't think it'd be all that hard, but I totally failed.

Mr. Dante had reserved a bunch of tables for us at this huge restaurant with a Mardi Gras theme. It was already packed when we got there, and our tables turned out to be spread out all over the restaurant. Since Owen and I were the first ones off the bus, we ended up in a booth with Trevor, Max, and Victoria. Which, of course, meant Warlock.

By the time the waitress set down our sodas and a basket of cheese biscuits, Trevor was already trying to convince Max he hadn't lost his last undead-warrior card last time we played. (Which was totally a lie—I remembered him losing it to Gabe.) Max didn't seem upset, though. More like amused. Now that I thought about it, since Max was pretty much the best Warlock player of all of us, he had to deal with most of Trevor's griping. And he was always really patient.

Victoria, on the other hand, seemed ready to argue Trevor into the ground.

"Gabe used his ice sword," she insisted. "You don't remember?"

"It wasn't an ice sword, it was a frozen dagger," Trevor retorted. "Totally different."

"Even if that was true—which it's *not*—the dagger gets your warrior anyway."

"Does not!"

Max sat next to Victoria, shuffling through his cards. It was funny—I'd seen them together a lot, mostly playing Warlock, but I'd never thought of them as a couple. They looked really cute together, though. I wondered if Victoria had kissed him yet, for Gabby's dare.

Max glanced up and caught me staring at him. "What?" he asked.

"Nothing!" I focused on my cards, trying not to smile. A second later, Victoria kicked me lightly under the table. I waited until Trevor finally conceded and it was Owen's turn before looking up at her. Raising an eyebrow, I glanced pointedly at Max. Victoria grinned and shook her head. *Not yet*, she mouthed.

When we got back to the hotel, I had to call Mom to check in—we'd only talked for a minute the first night of the trip because the reception was so bad in the gym. As soon as we hung up, I went next door to find Julia.

"I haven't seen her since dinner," said Brooke. She

and Leah were stretched out on the beds, watching a movie. Sophie sat on the floor, painting her toenails.

"Where's everybody else?" I asked.

Sophie glanced up. "I think Gabby's down the hall in room 1208," she told me. "Apparently Liam's mom bought a bunch of cupcakes. I don't know about the others, but a few people were still in the lobby when I went down a few minutes ago."

"Thanks." Grabbing my hoodie, I headed for the elevator. I figured I'd find Julia downstairs. Maybe Natasha had found her already. But when I got to the lobby, I didn't see either of them.

Owen was there, though, sitting on one of the sofas, sketchbook open in his lap. He smiled when I sat next to him, but flipped the page before I could see what he was working on.

"Why'd you come down here?" I rested my feet on the edge of the coffee table, taking care not to kick any of the colored pencils spread all over the surface.

"I wanted to work on some stuff, but there's a bunch of people playing Warlock in my room, and it got kind of loud," Owen replied. "What about you?"

"Looking for Julia and Natasha." I glanced around the lobby again. "No idea where they are. So what were you working on?"

"Just a few different sketches," he said, setting down a green pencil and picking up a brown one instead.

"Oh." I watched as he started shading in the tree

trunks in the gorilla picture. "Hey, were Max and Victoria in your room?"

He nodded. "Why?"

"Just curious." I glanced at him. "Did you know they're going to the spring dance together?"

"Um . . . no, I didn't."

The elevator doors opened. I looked up hopefully, but it was just Aaron and Liam. They headed straight for the vending machines.

"Maybe we could see if they want to have dinner before the dance," I said. "Max and Victoria. We could all ride together or something." When Owen didn't respond right away, I turned to face him. He was focused on the gorilla sketch, but his pencil wasn't moving. "Owen?"

Blink.

"You still want to go with me?" He sounded nervous again, like he had yesterday in the reptile house.

I sat up straight. "Of course! What makes you think I wouldn't?"

Blink, blink.

Cheeks flushed, Owen tapped the pencil on his knee. "Well, after what Natasha said yesterday, I thought maybe . . ." His gaze flickered over to the vending machines, and I realized what he meant.

Geez, first Gabby, now Owen. I almost laughed, but he looked really anxious, so I didn't.

"Okay, look," I said, glancing over at Aaron. "How awful would it be of me to ask him out after one of my best friends broke up with him? And besides, I already asked *you* to the dance! You don't really think I'd just change my mind like that, do you?"

Blink, blink, blink.

"Well, no," Owen said. "It's just . . . I know you like him, so if you—"

"I don't," I interrupted. "I don't like him anymore. Just as a friend."

He finally looked up, gray eyes wide with surprise. "You don't?"

I shook my head. "Nope."

"Oh. Okay." Owen picked up another pencil and went back to the gorilla sketch. His face was still a little pink, but he was smiling. After a second, I realized I was, too.

"Holly!"

We both looked up as Natasha stepped out of the elevator. She started toward us, noticed Aaron and Liam walking back from the vending machines, and veered around a sofa, her face suddenly red. Aaron followed Liam into the elevator, his eyes fixed on his shoes.

"Well," I said when Natasha sat next to me. "That was awkward."

She groaned, rubbing her eyes. "Tell me about it. Anyway, want to go talk to Julia?"

"Do you know where she is?"

"Yeah, there's a courtyard by the pool," Natasha said. "She's there—or at least, she was a few minutes ago. I saw her out the window."

"Let's go." I nudged Owen before standing up.

"Hey, this amusement park we're going to tomorrow is supposed to have a pretty creepy funhouse."

"Count me out," Natasha said immediately.

I laughed. "Obviously. But you're in, right?" I added, looking at Owen.

"Yup." His eyes widened. "Hey—alien funhouse?"

"Of *course*." I nodded emphatically. "Add it to the list."

Owen grinned. "Okay. See you tomorrow, Holly."

"See you."

Natasha and I headed down the hall, looking for the exit to the courtyard. "Alien funhouse?" she asked.

"For our science fair project," I explained. "We're designing an alien theme park." Natasha pressed her lips together, like she was trying not to laugh. I gave her a defiant look as we walked outside. "Hey, I don't care if that sounds dorky. It's actually a lot of fun."

But she shook her head. "That's not what I'm . . . never mind."

"What, then?"

Natasha smiled. "Nothing. Hey, is that Julia?"

I squinted in the direction she was pointing. "Yeah."

Julia sat on one of the benches lining the gate to the pool. The sign on the gate said CLOSED UNTIL MAY but all the lights in the pool area were on. At first I thought Julia was texting, but as we got closer, I realized she was reading a book. Her cell phone sat on her knee.

"Hi," I said, and she jumped.

"Oh!" Julia's eyes flickered from me to Natasha. "I

didn't hear you coming. Um . . . hi."

She closed her book as Natasha and I sat on either side of her. Natasha chewed her thumbnail, and I took a deep breath to speak. But Julia winced, like she was bracing herself, and I hesitated.

Maybe she felt like you guys were ganging up on her. That's what Gabby had said on the bus. And when I thought about it, I saw her point. Julia didn't feel like she could talk to either of us, so she'd confided in Sophie instead.

"You go first," I said after a second. They both looked at me funny.

"What?" asked Julia.

"Tell us what's bothering you." I tried to smile at her. "We'll listen, I promise."

Julia stared down at her knees. "Okay. Um . . ." She cleared her throat. "I really am sorry about the sleepover. I couldn't stop thinking about it the whole time I was at that concert. And what you said on the phone, that I was choosing Seth over you . . ." Swallowing, Julia glanced at me. "I felt really awful, Holly. I did."

My throat started aching a little bit, so I just nodded.

"Then after band on Monday, you both just . . ." Julia took a deep breath. "It was obvious you'd been talking about it. Not just the party, but about everything—that I talk about him too much, and . . ." She wiped her eyes quickly. "I guess it just hurt my feelings, that you'd been complaining about me, but neither of you ever said anything to me, and . . . I didn't know you felt that way."

"We didn't want to tell you at first," Natasha said. Her voice was all scratchy. "You were just excited about Seth, and we were happy for you. We should've—"

"No, but you were right." Julia smiled, even though tears were streaming down her face. "It hurt my feelings, but you were right, and I—I felt really guilty. I *have* been spending a lot of time with him, but I didn't realize that meant I barely saw you guys anymore. Or that I was missing out on so much. I mean, I didn't even know you were going to break up with Aaron."

Natasha's mouth fell open. "Wait—I *just* did that, like, an hour ago. Right after dinner. How did you even hear about it?"

"Sophie told me."

"I didn't tell Sophie!" Natasha exclaimed.

Julia wiped her eyes again. "She heard it from Liam."

I couldn't help giggling through my tears. "She might be a good listener, but she's an even better talker."

Natasha laughed. "I guess so."

"So what happened?" Julia asked. "Are you okay?"

"Yeah, I'm fine." Natasha shrugged. "It wasn't exactly the most fun conversation ever, but he didn't seem all that surprised." She smiled a little. "It would've been easier if he wasn't so nice. I still really like him, you know? We just don't have anything in common except band."

"Oh." Julia was quiet for a few seconds. "I'm sorry."

"It's okay."

"No, not about that," Julia said, then shook her head. "I mean, I *am* sorry about Aaron! But I'm also sorry for, you know . . . everything."

"It's okay." I smiled at her. "I'm sorry, too."

"Me too!" Natasha threw her arms around Julia, and so did I. We ended up in a crying, laughing, three-person hug on the bench, followed by a good minute of hiccuping and sniffling.

"We still want to hear about Seth, too," I told Julia, adjusting my ponytail. "Okay?"

She nodded. "Okay. And I want to hear about you and Owen."

"Okay." I paused, my hands still on my hair. "Wait—what are you talking about?"

"Come on, Holly," Julia said, grinning. "Maybe we haven't talked much in the last few weeks, but I'm not *blind*."

Natasha's eyes were wide. "Wait, what'd I miss?"

"I have no idea," I said honestly.

"I saw you guys walking around together," Julia told me. "Yesterday, at the zoo."

"So?"

Julia stared at me expectantly, but I just gave her a blank look. Sighing, she turned to Natasha.

"They were holding hands."

"Aw!" Beaming, Natasha reached over and socked me lightly on the arm. "Holly, you said you'd *tell* us if you liked Owen!"

"I would!" I exclaimed. My face felt warm. "That

wasn't . . . I mean, it's not like that. It was kind of an accident."

"An accident?" Julia repeated.

I nodded. "I was in a hurry when we got off the bus and I wasn't really thinking. I just grabbed his hand for a second so he'd walk fast, too, and then I . . . forgot."

Julia arched an eyebrow. "You forgot you were holding his hand?"

"Well, for a few minutes," I said. "But when I realized it, I figured it'd be rude if I just let go, so I . . . didn't."

It sounded like a lame reason, even to me. After a few seconds of silence, Julia and Natasha burst out laughing.

Sighing, I got to my feet. "Okay, so it's hard to explain," I told them. "But trust me, we're—"

"Just friends." Julia stood up and linked her arm with mine. "We know, we know."

They teased me all the way back to our rooms. I was so relieved everything was back to normal with Julia, I didn't even care. Although I couldn't help feeling grateful they didn't know about the accidental cuddling on the bus. I'd just keep that one to myself.

"Why did I let you talk me into this?"

I turned around to smile at Natasha. "Because you can't say you're afraid of roller coasters if you've never even been on one."

Our car lurched, and Natasha and Julia both shrieked. Next to me, Gabby's arms were already sticking straight up in the air.

"Here we go!" she yelled. Slowly, we moved backward along the track, which went from straight to vertical after a few seconds.

"Don't worry," I called over my shoulder. "It's just a hundred-foot drop or so to start with."

Julia groaned. "Thanks, Holly."

We reached the top, facing the ground, and the car was still for a few seconds.

"That churro probably wasn't a good idea," I told Gabby, glancing down at my all-region T-shirt. "I don't want you throwing up on me."

She grinned. “Please. I’ve never gotten sick on a—”

Then the car dropped, and everyone (including me and Gabby) screamed. The track twisted and turned, with so many loops and corkscrews that I lost count. After half a minute, our car went straight up the end of the track again, but now we were facing the sky.

“What’s going on?” Julia had her hands over her eyes.

I grinned. “We’re doing it again, but backward.”

“We’re doing it *again*?”

“It’s called the Rebound,” I said innocently. “What did you expect?”

“Holly, I swear to—”

But the car dropped again, and whatever Julia was going to say got lost in all the screaming. We plummeted down, then straight, then around all the loops and corkscrews again, only it was even scarier because we couldn’t see what was coming next. By the time we pulled back up to the platform, my heart was pounding wildly and my stomach felt like it was in my throat.

“That was *awesome*!” I exclaimed, following Gabby out of the car.

“Definitely,” she agreed. “And I need another churro.”

“Ew, you didn’t throw up the first one, did you?”

She looked confused. “No, I just want another one.”

We waited until Julia and Natasha joined us at the end of the platform. Natasha’s eyes were huge.

"Well?" I asked, waiting for her to yell at me for dragging her on a roller coaster.

She blinked a few times. Then a huge smile spread across her face. "I *loved* it!"

Julia and I gaped at her. "Seriously?"

"Yes!" Natasha hopped up and down a few times, beaming. "Let's go on it again. Oh wait, let's go to that one we passed earlier—the Brain Bender!"

"Yes!" Gabby exclaimed. "That's the one by the churro stand!" They hurried off the platform. Julia elbowed me as we followed.

"You created a monster," she said, still staring at Natasha in disbelief.

I grinned. "Good."

Four churros and three coasters later, we bought a round of slushy lemonades and crammed onto a bench by a fountain.

"Which one next?" Natasha asked, consulting a map. "Ooh, we haven't done Momentum yet, or the Splash—it's a water ride, but it still has a few drops. Or—"

"What's *happened* to you?" Julia cried, and I laughed.

"Or Silver Cyclone," Natasha finished. "So which one?"

"Actually, I'm supposed to meet Owen in fifteen minutes," I told her. "Why don't you come?"

"I'm *not* doing that funhouse."

"Come on," I said with a grin. "You thought you

were scared of roller coasters, and now you love them! Just give it a shot."

"Don't have to." Natasha pointed to the funhouse on the map. "Professor Loony's Funhouse."

"Yeah, so?"

She thrust the map in my face. "Professor Loony is a *clown*, Holly. A scary one. And I went to that horrible haunted house with you for Halloween. Those clowns were, like, the creepiest things ever."

Julia nodded vehemently in agreement. Slurping her lemonade, Gabby squinted at the picture.

"I don't get it. Clowns aren't scary at all," she said. "Hang on—what's wrong with his teeth? They're kind of . . . pointy."

"They kind of look like a vampire's," I agreed. "Which is totally different than the zombie clowns at that haunted house. They didn't even *have* teeth."

Natasha smacked my head with the map. "For the millionth time, that's *why* they were so creepy!"

After a few minutes of protesting, Julia and Natasha finally agreed to walk to the funhouse with us. A long line stretched from the entrance, which happened to look like the gaping mouth of a giant clown head. His teeth *were* pretty wicked-looking.

"Wait for me, okay?" Gabby asked. "I gotta find the restroom first."

"Okay." I scanned the line and spotted Aaron and Liam near the front. Trevor and Gabe weren't too far behind them, and Leah, Victoria, and Max were standing near the exit. “Are you sure you guys don’t want to come? It’s not a haunted house, it’s just—”

“Holly,” Julia said firmly. “Nothing you can say could possibly make me walk in that place. You couldn’t *pay* me to go in there. I wouldn’t go even if . . .” She trailed off, glancing behind me. “Hi, Owen!”

“Hi.” Owen appeared at my side, hands in his pockets. He was doing his confused blinking thing, probably because Julia and Natasha were smiling at him in a really goofy way. *Oh, for the love,* I thought, fighting the urge to tell them to knock it off.

“Gabby’s coming with us,” I told Owen instead. “But these two are chicken.”

“It’s true,” Julia agreed. “I’m not ashamed. Clowns are terrifying.”

“More roller coasters it is, then!” Natasha opened her map again. “But I still have to pick the next one.”

“Have you done Momentum yet?” asked Owen.

“No! Is it good?”

He nodded. “Really good. Gabe threw up.”

Natasha and I laughed, and she grabbed Julia’s hand. “Momentum it is!”

“My stomach needs a break!” Julia protested weakly, but she allowed Natasha to pull her away from the funhouse. “Bye, Holly! Bye, Owen,” she added, that goofy smile back on her face. Rolling my eyes, I turned to Owen.

“Should we get in line?” I asked. “Gabby’ll be out any second.”

"Sure!"

We stood behind a man and what looked like his two daughters. The youngest couldn't have been more than eight.

"Remind me to tell Julia and Natasha that third-graders are braver than they are," I said, and Owen laughed.

Gabby turned up with Leah, Victoria, and Max, who'd already been through the funhouse but wanted to go again. "This is my third time," Victoria said. "I'm not stopping until I make it through the barrel room without falling."

The line moved pretty quickly, and soon we were stepping inside. After the first minute, which involved climbing a narrow staircase, then sliding down a twisty slide that led to a dark room where a clown popped out from behind a trick wall, I was glad Julia and Natasha had chickened out. They'd probably be trying to climb back up the slide.

Next came a crooked maze, where some of the corridors got so narrow you couldn't walk through them anymore and had to turn back to find another way. When we finally got through it, Victoria turned and held her arms out to keep us all back. Behind her stretched a long, spinning tunnel.

"Barrel room," she announced. "I'll go first. The trick is to take it at a run."

"How would you know?" Max asked, grinning. "You've done it twice, and you fell both times."

"Because . . . ," Victoria said, hands on her hips. "Because be quiet, that's how."

We snickered as she turned and got into a runner's stance.

"Ready?" Gabby yelled. "Three, two . . . *one*!"

With a warrior cry, Victoria bolted into the tunnel. For a few seconds, it looked like she was going to make it straight through. Then she veered up the right side and tripped on her way down. She didn't fall, though—arms flailing wildly, she stumbled the last few steps out of the tunnel, crashed into the wall, and raised her arms in victory from the floor.

"Made it!" Victoria hollered, although everyone was laughing so hard we barely heard her.

Max went next, then Leah, both stumbling, falling, and getting up again until they reached the end. When Gabby's turn came, she took me and Owen by either arm without warning and pulled us in, too. We bumped into one another and the sides, but none of us fell. Then Gabby let go of our arms a few steps early and sprinted out of the tunnel. I grabbed Owen's hand before either of us could fall, and we barely made it out. This time, I let go right away.

"Close one," I said, trying to catch my breath.

He smiled. "Yeah."

We crossed a bridge made of stones that kept shifting, and ended up in a giant maze of distorted mirrors. After a minute of walking and making fun of our warped mirror images, Gabby turned around in a circle.

"We lost them." Cupping her hands over her mouth, she called: "*Victoria!*"

"Over here!" We followed the sound of Victoria's voice, but couldn't find her, Max, or Leah. Although just for a second, I did catch a glimpse of a clown reflection in one of the mirrors. There were probably a few creeping around the maze. Yeah, it was definitely a good thing that Julia and Natasha hadn't come in.

"Oh, hey!" Gabby poked me in the back. "I forgot about Nick—whatever happened with him? Did he call you?"

It took me a second to realize she was looking at all the names on the back of my all-region T-shirt.

"Um, yeah." I tried to sound nonchalant. "Once. But my stupid brother got on the phone after a few minutes, so we hung up."

Gabby was grinning. "But he called you! Did you get his number? You should—oh!" She clapped, and the sound echoed. "You should ask him to the dance!"

Oh, great. I shook my head quickly. "No, I don't—"

"Come *on*, Holly!" Gabby fell into step beside me. "He'd totally say yes—he liked you. And see if that friend of his is single. What was his name, Isaac? No, Ian. We could—"

"Gabby, I've already got a date."

She stopped in her tracks, grabbing my arm. "Wait, really? Who?"

Owen and I glanced at each other at the same time, our faces equally red. After a moment, Gabby's eyes widened in realization.

"*Oh.*" She turned and walked backward, facing us. A slow smile spread across her face. "Gotcha. Hmm."

Yup, this was stellar. Trapped in a hall of mirrors surrounded by infinite embarrassed Hollys and Owens and infinite teasing Gabbys.

Clearing her throat, Gabby looked at Owen. "So when did you ask her?"

Despite all of the awkwardness, I couldn't help but giggle. "What are you, a reporter?"

"No, ma'am, just a concerned citizen," Gabby replied with a grin. "Come on, Owen—spill. Did you just ask her today? Or was it before the trip?"

"Um . . ." Owen shot me a look that was part pleading, part apologetic.

"I asked him," I told Gabby. "Before winter break, actually."

"Before . . . seriously?" Gabby sputtered. "Wait, so you guys have been dating for, like, three months and you didn't even—"

"We're not dating."

She eyed me, then Owen. "You're not?"

We both shook our heads. Gabby turned back to me. "But—"

"Gabby," I interrupted, pointing. "You might want to turn around."

"Nice try. I just want to know if—"

"No, there's a seriously freaky-looking clown behind you."

"Carrying a giant pair of scissors," Owen added.

"Very funny," Gabby said. But her eyes flickered to the mirrors. When she saw the clown, she spun around with a horror movie–worthy scream, which quickly faded to a giggle. The clown's scissors and pointy teeth were obviously plastic. He lunged at Gabby, and Owen and I stepped to the side as she fled past us, yelling, "Please don't cut my hair, Mr. Scary Clown!" A few seconds after they both flew around the corner, I heard Victoria and Max laughing.

Owen and I grinned at each other. Then we both looked away. Which really wasn't very effective, since we were surrounded by mirrors. We couldn't *not* see ourselves.

"Sorry about that," I said at last. "Gabby's kind of nosy."

"It's okay." He shrugged and gave me a small smile. "I don't mind."

We wandered through the mirrors, following the sound of Gabby's yells. "So how much longer will you have baseball after school?" I asked, desperate for anything other than awkward silence. "I miss *Prophets*."

"Me too," Owen said. "Just three more weeks of baseball. But there's no practice Monday, if you want to come over. Trevor's coming, too," he added quickly.

"Definitely!" I grinned. "It's been a while since I've beaten Trevor at anything other than Warlock."

He laughed. We spent the rest of the funhouse talking about stuff like our alien project and which movies we should watch on the bus ride home. And when we finally found the exit and Gabby greeted us with "Hiya, lovebirds!" neither of us even blushed.

Okay, maybe we did a little bit. But the teasing really didn't seem to bother Owen, which was a relief. It didn't matter what anyone else thought, as long as we knew we were just friends.

Unless the teasing didn't bother him for a different reason.

I squinted in the sunlight as we left the funhouse. Owen was next to me, talking to Max about which ride we should go on next. Was it possible he actually *did* like me? He didn't seem to mind holding hands.

Overthinking things again, I told myself firmly. *Not minding* when someone grabbed your hand was a lot different than *wanting* to actually hold hands with them. And besides, it had been humiliating enough last semester when I thought Aaron liked me. Owen was one of my best friends—no way I'd make that mistake with him. If he really did like me, I'd probably know.

Our last night in New Orleans was interesting. By nine thirty, Natasha had run up and down the hall with Sophie riding piggyback, Julia's hair was sticking up like a mad scientist (thanks to almost an entire can of hairspray) and Leah had eaten an impressive nineteen Twizzlers in one minute. We'd been playing truth or dare for half an hour, and no one had picked truth yet.

"How much longer?" Brooke asked from the corner. She was in a headstand, her feet propped against the wall for balance.

"Until the next person's turn is up," Gabby replied. Brooke made a noise that sounded like half-groan, half-giggle.

"Well, hurry up! All the blood's rushing to my head."

"I warned you guys," Victoria said. She was still teasing and combing Julia's hair. "Gabby's dares can be brutal."

"Hey, the last one I gave you worked out pretty well," Gabby pointed out, waggling her eyebrows.

Victoria grinned. "Well, that's true."

"Gabby!" Brooke yelled. Her face was turning red. "Who's next?"

"Let's see . . ." Gabby tapped her chin, but her eyes flickered in my direction. "Holly . . . truth or dare?"

I didn't hesitate. "Truth."

Victoria glanced at me. "Are you sure? Her truths are usually worse than her dares."

But I saw the devious smile on Gabby's face, and I knew exactly what her dare would be. And I was so not about to go kiss Owen on a dare. "Definitely. Truth."

Gabby sighed. "Okay, fine. But you have to be *honest*."

Shrugging, I handed Victoria another package of barrettes. "I promise." I already knew what Gabby would ask. And sure enough:

"Do you like Owen?"

Everyone giggled. "Do you?" Brooke beamed at me, which looked funny considering she was upside down. "Aw, you two would be such a cute couple!"

"Thanks," I said, smiling. "But nope, we're just friends."

"Holly," Gabby said seriously. "Truth or dare is not to be taken lightly. If you're lying, you'll have seven years of bad luck, and a herd of angry goats will eat all your socks. Something like that, anyway—I don't really know the rules."

I laughed. "I'm telling the truth, I swear!"

Gabby turned to Julia. "Is she lying?"

Julia glanced up at me and grinned. "She doesn't *think* she's lying."

"She's in denial," Natasha agreed, patting my head. I stuck my tongue out in response.

"Okay. Let's look at the facts." Gabby stuck out her hand and began counting off points on her fingers. "One: you asked him to the spring dance, like, a *decade* early. Two: you hang out with him all the time. And three . . ." She paused, brow furrowed. "Three: you obviously like each other. So there."

I just smiled and shook my head. The teasing only went on for another minute before Brooke yelled, "She's telling the truth, okay?" and fell over, accidentally kicking a chair and causing Sophie to spill an entire box of crackers all over the floor.

"Next dare!" Gabby cried. "Human vacuum. Whose turn is it?"

𝄞

Julia's hair was still sticking up all over the place the next morning. "I didn't have time to wash it," she mumbled, rubbing her eyes. "Why didn't you wake me up earlier?"

"I tried," I told her. "Next time I'll get the air horn."

Rolling her eyes, Julia slid into a seat a few rows back from the front. When I tried to sit next to her, Natasha grabbed the back of my shirt.

“That’s my spot,” she said with a grin. “You should sit with Owen.”

Sighing, I glanced out the window and caught a glimpse of blond hair. “Fine, but seriously, you guys . . .” I turned, tossing my backpack into the seats opposite them. “Quit acting all weird around him, okay? You’re going to freak him out.”

“Okay, okay.” Julia grinned at me. “We’ll behave ourselves.”

They did, too. Mostly. A few times while we watched *Project Centaurus,* I caught them giggling. Probably because Owen and I were debating the plot again, since this was the third time we’d seen it. (I thought the idea of a robot feeling emotions was ridiculous, because then it wouldn’t be a robot anymore. Owen argued that a really advanced robot maybe *could* feel emotions but that wouldn’t make it human. Whatever.)

After lunch, I split my Warlock cards with Julia and taught her how to play. She seemed kind of wary until, to everyone’s surprise, she scored Max’s silent-scepter card. Then she really got into it.

“You’re good at card games, Natasha loves roller coasters . . .” Shuffling my deck, I shook my head. “Horror movies are next, I swear. You’ll both end up coming with me to see the sequel to *House of the Wicked* in May.”

“Not in a million years,” Julia said. Her lips twitched as she studied her cards. “I bet Owen’ll go with you, though.”

I gave her the side-eye, and she and Natasha snickered. Owen glanced up.

"Yeah, I'll go," he said immediately. "The first one was really cool."

"Okay." I handed Julia a cursed-vault card and pretended not to see the two of them wearing those goofy smiles again.

Unfortunately, the bus made it all the way back to Millican without any problems. No potential encounters with zombie farmers this time. Although I had new appreciation for the frigid air conditioning, especially since Trevor's shoes stayed on. Owen spent the last few hours sketching, while Julia, Natasha, and I made plans to have a belated birthday sleepover for Julia that night. When we pulled into the parking lot, I glanced out the window and grinned.

"Seth's here," I told Julia. Her face lit up.

Mrs. Park insisted everyone clean up the inside of the bus before we unloaded, which was a good call, to be honest. Let's just say not everyone was capable of spending over nine hours on a bus without making a pretty ridiculous mess. (It was easy to spot Gabby's seat, thanks to the M&M's scattered all over the floor.)

"Oh *man*," I cried when I stepped off the nice, clean bus. "I have to ride home in the trash mobile?" Natasha laughed when she saw Chad's car on the other side of the parking lot. We lagged behind Julia, who was already hugging Seth and talking a mile a minute.

"Is the inside really that bad?" Natasha asked.

"Last time my mom drove it, she spent half the day at work with a wrapper covered in melted chocolate stuck to the back of her skirt until her boss told her," I said, and Natasha wrinkled her nose, laughing. "Hi, Seth!"

"Hi!" Seth smiled at me. "I brought you something. Since you liked those Edgar Allan Poe stories, I thought maybe you'd like these, too." He held out a book called *Great Tales of Horror,* by H. P. Lovecraft.

"Awesome!" I flipped through it eagerly. "Thanks!"

"You're welcome." He turned to Julia. "So do you want to come over for dinner tonight? My sister's here this weekend—she said she'd take us to Spins."

"Oh, um . . ." Julia tucked her hair behind her ear. "Actually, I'm spending the night at Holly's. Kind of a belated birthday party. How about lunch tomorrow instead?"

"Sure!"

Glancing across the parking lot, I noticed Owen's whole family had come to pick him up. Mrs. Grady was handing him a big yellow envelope—even from here, it was easy to see she was really excited about something.

"See you guys tomorrow, okay?" I hurried over to Owen, dragging my suitcase behind me. He was staring at a piece of paper and blinking. A *lot.*

"Hi, Holly!" Mrs. Grady beamed at me.

"Hi!" I waited for Owen to look up, but he seemed sort of paralyzed. "What's going on?"

"Apparently, he entered an art contest and didn't

tell anyone," said Mrs. Grady. She didn't sound at all upset—in fact, she sounded proud. "*And* . . . go on, tell her!" She nudged Owen's arm, but he didn't move.

Megan sighed loudly and impatiently. "He *won*!" she cried, thrusting her fist in the air.

"He's one of five winners," Mrs. Grady interjected quickly. "They've invited him to a workshop in San Antonio!"

"*Owen*!" I yelled, throwing my arms around him. "I knew it! I *told* you!"

Red-faced, Owen laughed and hugged me back. His mom was still talking.

"The letter says there were hundreds of entries. *And* Owen is the youngest winner—I spoke to the contest coordinator on the phone. She said the judges were really impressed, and—"

"Okay, Mom." Owen's face seriously could not get any redder, but he was smiling.

"It's pretty amazing," Steve said, and I was pleased to see he looked proud, too. "Why didn't you tell us you entered?"

Owen shrugged. "I don't know . . . I guess I figured it was a long shot."

"When's the workshop?" I asked, bouncing up and down on my toes. Owen read the letter again.

"The weekend after next." He looked at Mrs. Grady. "Is that okay? It says they provide rooms and food and everything, but we'll still have to drive there."

"Of course it's okay!" Mrs. Grady exclaimed, while

Steve leaned over to peer at the letter.

"Hang on . . . the first day is a Friday," he said. "That's the second-to-last baseball game."

Mrs. Grady waved her hand. "We'll talk to the coach about it. I'm sure he'll understand if Owen misses one game for something this important."

"I think he would." Owen swallowed. "And, um . . . there's something I need to tell you guys."

I held my breath.

"I don't like baseball," he said. "I'm not going to quit or anything, but—but I don't want to try out again next year. Or for basketball, or anything else. I just . . . I don't like sports. Sorry," he added, staring at his shoes.

Mrs. Grady shook her head. "Owen, you have nothing to apologize for. Right, Steve?"

I watched Steve's face carefully. He looked surprised. Surprised, but not upset or angry.

"Right," he said after a moment. "I didn't realize you felt that way about it, Owen. I shouldn't have pushed you so hard to try out."

Owen's shoulders sagged in relief. "It's okay."

"Besides," Mrs. Grady added, tapping the letter. "You need to focus on this! Did you read about the workshop?"

"Yeah, it's about animation right?" I asked eagerly, leaning close to look.

"Yeah." Owen scanned the letter again. "The basics of animated videos—cartoons and stuff like that."

"*Whoa.*" I stared at him. "Hey, maybe you could do

something like that for our science fair project! You know, make like a cartoon Alien Park commercial or something."

He grinned. "Maybe!"

After I said good-bye to Owen and his family, I grabbed my luggage and headed over to the trash mobile.

"About time!" Chad watched in the rearview mirror as I gingerly placed my suitcase on the pile of napkins and soda cans covering the backseat. "Mom and Dad went to some craft show after lunch and got stuck in traffic coming home."

"Thanks for cleaning the car for me," I said as sarcastically as possible, setting my horn case on the floor.

"You're welcome for picking you up," Chad replied just as sarcastically. "Hurry up, okay? I've got to be at work in an hour."

"All right, all right."

I shut the back door and heard someone call my name. Turning, I saw Owen hurrying across the parking lot.

"What's up?" I asked when he reached me.

"Um . . ." Owen paused, like he wasn't sure what to say. His cheeks were flushed, and his eyes were bright. "Just . . . well, thank you. You know, for making me enter that contest. And for convincing me to tell my parents I hate baseball," he added, and I laughed.

"You're welcome."

I waited, because he looked like he wanted to say something else. And after a moment's hesitation, Owen held out the big yellow envelope. "This is for you."

I took it, confused. "Is this the stuff about the workshop?"

"No, I took all that out to use the envelope." Owen stuck his hand in his pockets. "It's kind of a thank-you present, I guess."

"Holly, come on!"

Looking down, I was horrified to see Chad sticking his head out of the passenger window. He squinted at the envelope in my hands, then eyed Owen suspiciously. "Hey."

Owen blinked. "Um, hi."

Sighing, Chad arched an eyebrow. "Okay, Holly. Which one's this?"

"Chad, this is my friend Owen. Owen, this is my brother, Chad. Okay, we're done here." Placing my palm flat on Chad's face, I pushed him back inside the car.

"Hey, it's my right to interrogate this guy!" His voice sounded muffled against my hand. "Especially if he's the one with half my movies."

"Knock it off!" I hissed, then turned to face Owen. "Sorry."

He looked rather terrified. "It's okay. I'll see you Monday. *Prophets* after school, right?"

"Definitely."

With a last smile, Owen turned and headed back to his mom's car. Opening the door, I brushed all the empty cartons and wrappers off my seat and sat down.

"Finally," Chad muttered.

"You know what?" I said, buckling my seatbelt. "You really don't have to try and scare every guy I know to death."

"Why not? It's fun terrorizing your boyfriends."

I rolled my eyes. "Chad, you do know that just because I'm friends with a boy, it doesn't make him my boyfriend, right?"

"Whatever you say."

Once Chad had turned up the radio, I opened the yellow envelope. Inside was a single, thick sheet of paper. I pulled it out carefully and gasped.

"What's that?" Chad glanced over, but I didn't answer.

The white alligator sketch. Owen had colored the habitat—all the different shades of green in the water and the bluish-gray rocks made the alligators look even more ghostlike. But there was something else, something I hadn't seen when I'd watched him draw it because his hand kept blocking the right side of the page.

It was *me*.

I mean, I couldn't see my face, but it was obviously me. Standing in front of the habitat, hair in a ponytail, red hoodie, hands in my pockets. I remembered how mesmerized I'd been, watching the alligators. And that whole time, Owen had been sitting behind me, drawing the whole thing. I pictured the intent expression he always got when he worked on a sketch and felt a funny little flutter in my chest.

"Hang on." Chad leaned over to look, and I realized we were at a stoplight. "Is that you?"

"Yeah." I tucked the drawing back into the envelope to keep it safe from all the greasy cartons and dirty napkins.

Chad was still staring. "Did that guy *draw* that?"

"Yeah."

"And he gave it to you?"

"Yeah."

After a few seconds of silence, Chad let out an unimaginably loud snort. "Oh no, he's not your boyfriend. Yeah ri—"

"Green light," I interrupted, pointing. Then I cranked up the radio as loud as I could stand it. Chad was still laughing at me, but at least now I couldn't hear him.

I wasn't all that irritated, though. Actually, I felt kind of giddy. Tapping my fingers on the envelope, I wondered what Julia and Natasha would say tonight when they saw Owen's sketch. There would be more teasing, more jokes about crushes, more goofy smiles. But I wouldn't mind.

Actually, I realized with a smile, I couldn't wait to show them.

Acknowledgments

Thank you to my editor, fellow band geek, and cabaret artist extraordinaire Jordan Hamessley for reliving countless Texas band stories with me. And enormous thanks to editor in chief Sarah Fabiny for all her support.

Thank you to Sarah Davies—superagent, hippie guitarist, support counselor, and all-around amazing person.

Thank you to art director Giuseppe Castellano, designer Mallory Grigg, and illustrator Genevieve Kote for making this series sparkle.

Thank you to production editor Rebecca Behrens for her keen eye, for teaching my clueless self what "stet" means, and most likely for catching mistakes on this very acknowledgments page.

Thank you to Amanda Hannah, Kate Hart, Kirsten Hubbard, and Kaitlin Ward, for all the things.

Thank you to my parents, John and Mary, and my sister, Heather, for being band supporters for the last twenty-something years.

Thank you to Josh, for constantly encouraging me with both writing and music. Thank you to Adi, for singing along.

And thank you to any bus driver who has ever worked a band trip. Heroes, all of you.

Coming Soon!

#4 Crushes,
Codas, and Corsages

Turn the page for a sneak peek!

"Doesn't count."

"Does so."

Julia glared at me, twirling the combination on her locker. "Does not. I cannot *believe* I let you talk me into watching that movie."

I grinned. "Hey, I gave you fair warning. And there was plenty of romantic junk."

"Holly, for the last time . . ." Shaking her head, Julia started cramming books into her backpack. "It doesn't count as a kissing scene when the guy's eyes turn black and *bees come out of his mouth*."

"Wow, which movie's that?"

Julia and I turned, startled. Aaron Cook smiled at us as he opened his locker, which was right next to Julia's.

"*Dark Omnibus*. It's pretty good," I told him, right as Julia said, "It's *horrible*."

Aaron laughed. "Mixed reviews."

"*Horrible*," Julia hissed again, and I giggled.

"How was your spring break?" Aaron asked.

"Pretty good," I replied. "Went to the lake with my parents and brother. Nothing too exciting. How about you?"

"It was all right." Aaron caught several folders and books as they tumbled out of his locker. "Spent a few days in Austin with my older sister and her family. And—" He stopped, a weird look on his face, and I turned around.

"Hi!" Natasha was smiling, but she looked uncomfortable, too. Slamming her locker shut, Julia spun around with a squeal and threw her arms around Natasha.

"How was your trip? What time did you get back? Did you get my message last night? We kept texting you, but I guess you were still on the plane, and then Holly made me watch this *horrible* movie, and I'm totally traumatized and—"

Laughing, I pushed her away. "Julia, get a grip!" I hugged Natasha, then glanced at Aaron, who looked pretty focused on shoving his jumble of folders back into his locker. Aaron and Natasha had been dating ever since winter break, but she'd broken up with him on the band trip to New Orleans. A nice break-up, not like a fight or anything. But still a break-up.

Aaron finally got his locker closed, then gave us all a quick smile. "See you guys in band!" he said before taking off down the hall.

"See you." I turned to see Natasha fidgeting nervously with the strap on her backpack. "Well. That was awkward."

She made a face. "Yeah. Sorry."

"I'm sure it'll get better," Julia said. "Don't you think?"

Natasha sighed. "I hope so—I mean, we're going to see each other every day in band. I hope he doesn't hate me."

"He doesn't hate you," I assured her. "I'm sure things will go back to normal soon. So how was Florida?"

"It was amazing!" Beaming, Natasha pulled out her phone and started flicking through photos. "Check it out! I took one of every roller coaster I rode."

My eyes widened as she scrolled past what looked like a creepy old hotel. "Hang on—you actually went on *that* ride?"

Natasha nodded proudly. "Yup! You'd love it."

Grabbing Natasha's phone, Julia groaned. "Oh my God, is that, like, a haunted house? What happened to the girl who was properly scared to death of all this stuff, like me?"

"It's not a haunted house—it's a drop ride," Natasha explained. "You know, where you free-fall. Although it *was* pretty creepy, too," she added as an afterthought. "The lights flicker on and off, and the elevator goes black right before it drops. You should've seen my parents' faces when I got in line. Actually, my whole family was kind of shocked."

“This is your fault.” Julia poked me in the shoulder. “You dragged her onto that roller coaster in New Orleans. You created this monster.”

Still scrolling through the photos, Natasha bounced on her toes. “I started making a list of amusement parks we should go to this summer,” she told me, just as the bell rang.

Grinning, I picked up my backpack. “Awesome. Maybe we can find a good haunted drop ride for Julia.”

“Nooo . . . ,” Julia moaned. I waved as Natasha dragged her down the hall to their history class.

𝄞

When the bell rang to end third period, I bolted from the gym to the band hall so fast I probably broke my own sprinting record in PE. The chair test results were posted outside on Mr. Dante’s office door.

FRENCH HORN

Natasha Prynne

Holly Mead

Owen Reynolds

Brooke Dennis

Relieved, I headed to the cubby room. Natasha and I were competing constantly for first chair. It was a friendly rivalry, though. I still had another chair test before the end of the year—I could try for first chair one more time. And besides, I wasn’t exactly bummed about sitting next to Owen.

A few kids already were getting their instruments.

I waved to Victoria Rios, who already had her trumpet out. She was talking to Max Foster near the trombone section's cubbies. Just as I was closing my case, I heard a couple familiar voices.

"I'm telling you, it's not cheating. It's just adjusting the rules a little."

"Swapping half of your deck in the middle of a game is cheating, Trevor."

Shoving my case back into my cubby, I hurried to the entrance. "Owen!"

Owen's eyes lit up. "Hi, Holly!" We had a brief, weird moment of almost hugging but just standing there smiling at each other like dorks instead. Then I thought *what the heck* and hugged him anyway, which was kind of awkward since I still had my horn.

"Hi, Holly," Trevor Wells said pointedly.

"Hey, Trevor," I said before turning back to Owen. "Okay, tell me about San Antonio! How was the workshop?"

Rolling his eyes, Trevor headed for his cubby. Owen's cheeks flushed as he pulled his sketchbook out of his backpack.

"It was great! Most of the work I did was computer animation, but I've got some stuff here. And I had a lot of ideas for our science project. Maybe—"

The bell rang, cutting him off.

"Show me at lunch?" I asked, and he nodded.

"Sure!"

While Owen went to his cubby, I headed to my

seat and found Natasha sitting next to it with a rather nervous expression. Aaron sat directly behind her, talking to Liam Park. I gave Natasha a sympathetic smile as I slipped past her to my chair. Hopefully Julia was right and things would get less awkward between Natasha and Aaron soon.

"What's this?" I picked up a brochure on my chair. "Oh . . . Lake Lindon."

"I think Mr. Dante put them on everyone's chairs before the bell," Natasha said, pointing to the brochure she'd set on her music stand. Lake Lindon Band Camp was a whole week of band-geek heaven—cabins, rehearsals, a concert, all kinds of stuff. It was where Julia and Natasha had met last summer.

"Any chance your parents will let you go this year?" Natasha asked hopefully.

Sighing, I stuck the brochure in my backpack. "Last year, they said I could go the summer before high school. But I'm definitely going to ask again."

"Hiya, ladies." Gabby Flores flopped into the chair on Natasha's other side, still tightening the mouthpiece on her saxophone. "Holly, I'm still freaking out about my paper."

I nodded in agreement. Gabby and I had first-period English together, and this morning Mr. Franks had given us back our first drafts for this huge research project he'd assigned back in January. Everyone's papers had been covered in red marks and scribbled notes.

"Seriously, I'm going to have to rewrite the whole

thing," Gabby said. "And it's due next week? He's crazy. How'd yours look? Hi, Owen," she added.

Shrugging, I scooted my chair back a little to let Owen pass me. "He said I need more sources. There are a lot more notes, but I haven't read them all yet."

I tried to keep my voice light, but I was already kind of stressing about the rest of the semester, and my first day back wasn't even halfway over. Between the research project, the science fair, and final exams, my countdown to summer was starting to feel more like a deadline time bomb.

Something Mr. Dante didn't help one bit when, after warm-ups, he handed out a letter for our parents. *University Interscholastic League Concert and Sight-Reading Contest* was printed in bold along the top. I scanned it quickly, even though he'd talked to us about most of this earlier in the semester. A bus would take us to Ridgewood High School for the contest after first period, so our parents didn't have to worry about driving. We'd perform on stage for three judges, and they'd each give us a rating. Then we'd go to another room to sight-read a piece of music, and three more judges would rate us on that. After we got our ratings, we'd go to Spins for a pizza lunch . . . and, hopefully, to celebrate.

In the back of the band hall was a long shelf lined with trophies. Those were for Sweepstakes, which meant earning a Superior rating from all six judges on stage *and* in sight-reading. Millican had a lot of them, but not for every single year—I'd already looked. I *really* wanted us to add another trophy this year.

Mr. Dante began moving through the rows, placing a sheet of music facedown on everyone's stands. Leaning to my left, I nudged Brooke Dennis.

"You guys got Sweepstakes last year, right?" I whispered. Brooke was in eighth grade and had been in Advanced Band last year, too.

She nodded. "Mrs. Wendell was really excited, since it was her last year. I think that was the fifth time in a row we got Sweepstakes."

My stomach twinged with nerves. Mrs. Wendell had been the band director at Millican practically forever, but she'd retired last year. I wondered if Mr. Dante was anxious about UIL, too, since it was his first year teaching here. If he was, he sure didn't show it.

"Let's talk a bit about sight-reading," Mr. Dante said cheerfully, placing a sheet of music on Liam's stand. "Yes, Gabby?"

Gabby lowered her hand. "What's the point of them judging us on music we've never even seen before? Especially since we've already been practicing the other songs so much."

"That *is* the point." Mr. Dante handed music to the percussionists. "The music we sight-read will be quite a bit easier that our other music. But it's a way for the judges to hear how good our fundamentals are—tone, rhythms, technique. I want to try it today, so there are a few rules we need to go over."

He stepped back up to the podium and started

to explain the process. After a minute, my eyes were pretty much bulging out of my head.

The judges would set a timer. Mr. Dante would have a few minutes to talk to us about the music, but he couldn't sing melodies or clap rhythms. Then the timer would go off, and he'd get another few minutes where he *could* sing or clap rhythms, but we still couldn't.

We couldn't play at *all*, just move our fingers along while he conducted. If we accidentally played a note or something, we actually could get disqualified. And when the timer went off again, we'd just . . . perform it. The entire song, without stopping, for the first time.

The whole thing was confusing, not to mention terrifying.

I glanced around the room. Most of the seventh-graders looked as anxious as I felt, but the eighth graders didn't. And they'd done this last year. Maybe it wasn't as scary as it sounded.

"Let's give it a shot." Mr. Dante set a timer, then opened his score. "Go ahead and turn over your music."

I flipped the page over. Well, it *did* look a little easier than our other music. I tapped my fingers on the valves while Mr. Dante talked us through it, stopping occasionally to point out difficult parts and remind us about the coda—a separate, final few measures at the bottom of the page.

When the timer went off, I glanced at Natasha. She shrugged.

"Looks easy enough," she whispered, and I nodded.

Mr. Dante raised his hands, and everyone sat up to play. At first, we sounded pretty good. We made it through almost half the page with just a few wrong notes and one misplaced cymbal crash.

Then the trumpets came in a few beats early, and their melody didn't line up with the clarinets.

Then all the saxophones except Gabby missed a key change, and she insistently squawked the right notes louder and louder.

Then literally, like, half the band missed a repeat sign while the French horn part only had rests, so all four of us lost count and didn't know when to come back in.

I was completely freaking out, my eyes darting back and forth between the music and Mr. Dante. He looked perfectly calm, cueing sections that sounded lost and gesturing for Gabby to stop honking. For a minute, we actually did start to play together again. But I only just remembered about the coda in time. I skipped down to the last line and played the last few measures, finishing just as Mr. Dante lowered his baton.

Most of the band was still going. They stopped pretty fast when they realized he wasn't conducting anymore.

"Okay, guys," Mr. Dante said, smiling around at us. Seriously, *how* was he still so calm? "Can someone tell me what it says above measure ninety-eight? Sophie?"

"'To coda,'" Sophie Wheeler replied.

"Right," Mr. Dante agreed. "So where *is* the coda? Holly?"

I squinted at my music and found the coda symbol.

"Measure one-twelve."

"Exactly." Mr. Dante nodded. "So after we take that repeat, we play through until we see 'to coda,' and then we jump down to that symbol. I'll do my best to cue you, but you have to watch out for those signs." Opening his folder, Mr. Dante pulled out another score. "Let's take out 'Labyrinthine Dances,' please."

"That's it?" Gabby blurted out. "We're not going to work on this one anymore?"

Mr. Dante smiled. "Sight-reading, Gabby. One shot. We'll be sight-reading several times a week until UIL, but it'll be a different piece every time. So tomorrow, we'll address some of the problems we ran into today, and give it another try with a new song."

Natasha and I exchanged nervous glances. He was right—one shot. And if that had been our sight-reading performance at UIL, no way would we get a Sweepstakes trophy.

Half an hour so wasn't long enough for lunch. Between everyone catching up after spring break, plus resuming our ongoing Warlock card game, we could've used at *least* an hour. And my fried brain really needed more of a rest before facing more projects and final-exam preparation.

I sat crammed in between Owen and Natasha. Owen, Trevor, and Max were already swapping cards over their sandwiches with several other Warlock players. On my right, Natasha was holding her phone across the table to show Seth her Disney pictures. Next to him, Julia glanced at a photo and started choking on her cookie.

"Hang on," she sputtered, grabbing the phone. "Is that—you went *bungee jumping*?"

"What?" I cried, looking up from my Warlock cards. Natasha shook her head.

"No, it wasn't really bungee jumping," she said. "More like a slingshot. You get strapped into this thing that's attached to two giant towers, and then you get pulled back and . . . catapulted."

"That's *awesome*," Seth told her, right as Julia said, "That's *insane*."

"I was kind of nervous," Natasha admitted. "But I promised myself I'd go on any ride that looked scary. And it's over really fast, too—way faster than a roller coaster." She grinned. "It was like flying. So cool. I'd definitely do it again."

I smiled. This was the happiest I'd seen Natasha since . . . well, maybe ever. At the beginning of the year we didn't even like each other. And even after we were friends, things were weird between us because we both liked Aaron. Then she'd started dating him, and while she seemed happy, it had been more of a nervous kind of happy. Like during lunch, when she used to go sit with Aaron and his friends and I'd get the feeling she'd almost rather stay with us.

Out of habit, I glanced over at Aaron's table. He was laughing and talking to some freckled eighth-grade girl I vaguely recognized. Wait . . . were they holding hands? I squinted, but then she stood to take her tray to the trash, and I wasn't sure if I'd imagined it.

Maybe Aaron was already dating someone else. If so, I hoped Natasha wouldn't be too upset.

"Your turn, Holly."

Looking up, I realized Owen and the other Warlock players were waiting expectantly. "Oh!" I glanced from the pile of cards in the center of the table to my own deck, then tossed a chimney-gnome card down. "Hey, I still want to see what you worked on in San Antonio," I told Owen as Erin Peale used a cursed-broom card to snag my gnome. His expression brightened.

"Oh, right!" Setting his cards down, Owen opened his backpack. I glanced over to make sure Julia wasn't giving me any goofy faces like she usually does around Owen, but she and Seth still were looking at Natasha's photos.

Owen opened his sketchbook. "So we started with motion sketches—drawing a character going through one motion. See?"

I burst out laughing. Twenty stick figures holding baseball bats covered the sheet in four neat rows. From left to right, I could see the progression as a ball zoomed towards the stick figure and he swung the bat and . . . missed. Which, I had to admit, happened more often then not when Owen was on the JV team. He hated baseball, but tried out just to make his parents happy.

"The workshop got me out of the last game," Owen said with a grin. "I figured this was a good tribute."

Snickering, I flipped through several more motion sketches. When I got to a page filled with waddling penguins, I stopped. "These don't look like yours."

Owen glanced down. "Oh yeah—Ginny drew some of this stuff."

"Ginny?"

"My partner," Owen explained. "They put everyone in pairs to work on the final project."

"Oh." I nodded, doing my best to look indifferent. But imagining this Ginny person drawing penguins in Owen's sketchbook was kind of irritating. When I flipped the page, the penguins all were paired up and dancing.

Make that *very* irritating.

The bell rang, and I handed Owen his sketchbook. "So you guys made an actual cartoon?"

"Yeah!" Owen gathered up his Warlock cards. "I'll show you on Thursday. If you're still coming over after school, I mean."

"Definitely." I stuffed my cards in my backpack. "I bet we're going to have lots of work to do on Alien Park."

Alien Park was our science fair project—kind of

like *Jurassic Park,* but with aliens instead of dinosaurs. I wasn't wrong about the work, either. When we got to science class, Mrs. Driscoll handed back our project outlines. And just like Mr. Franks with the research papers, she'd probably gone through a whole pack of red pens.

"Revisions due next Monday," she said, and I sighed. Sometimes I wondered if our teachers forgot we actually had other classes. Mrs. Driscoll spent most of the class period going over the new unit we were starting, on organisms and their environments, but I was kind of distracted. By Ginny and her stupid dancing penguins.

"So let's talk about habitats," Mrs. Driscoll was saying. "Some animals live in rainforests, others live in deserts, and some even in live the Arctic. We're going to take a look at their physical characteristics, as well as things like shelter and food available in their habitats . . ."

Owen leaned over. "This could help with our project. Like the Mars habitat," he whispered.

I nodded, and he started taking notes. After a few minutes, I realized I hadn't heard a word Mrs. Driscoll had said. And instead of notes, I'd doodled a penguin. But it just looked like a football with a beak.

About the Author

Michelle Schusterman is a former band director and forever band geek, starting back in the sixth grade when she first picked up a pair of drumsticks. Now she writes books, screenplays, and music in New York City, where she lives with her husband (and bandmate) and their chocolate Lab (who is more of a vocalist).